HIS CHOSEN MATE

HIS CHOSEN MATE

Six Pack Shifters

By
Julie Trettel

Thanks and Acknowledgments

For years I have been asked when I was going to write a human shifter romance, well, you've asked for it, you've waited, but wait no more. I know some of you are nervous while others very excited, but I couldn't be happier with how this story turned out and I truly hope you enjoy it too.

Thank you for always sticking with me. Happy reading!

James

Chapter 1

It was just another day on the job of what had turned into my pathetic, mundane life.

"Sheriff, looks like they're moving forward with charges against the boys and the movie theater instance."

"Goddamn it. Are you serious?"

"Yeah, looks like there's a new officer in town and he's convinced the district attorney they have a case."

"Get on the phone with Mr. Terrence and see if we can shut this shit down before it escalates any further. Have they set a hearing date yet?"

"Yes. Next week. Clearly, they aren't that worried about this case. It's low priority on the docket right now."

"Who'd they assign to it?"

"Judge Carter."

I groaned.

"What? I thought he liked you."

"Oh, he does, to an extent."

"Because you dated his daughter?"

"Something like that," I grumbled as he left my office to take a call in the next room.

Alone, I tried not to let myself think about that time in my life. Katherine Carter was pigheaded, stubborn, and argumentative. Being with her had been a true whirlwind and some of the happiest days of my life.

She was my everything, but she'd made it clear that she wasn't interested in marriage, or a long-term commitment, and I wanted to claim her for life.

I had even been ready to give up everything: my life in the Pack, my family, my chosen brotherhood with the Six Pack, everything. I was even willing to renounce who and what I was to be with this woman and my wolf was a hundred percent onboard with the plan. As far as he was concerned, she was it for us.

And then she'd broken my heart with her declaration for independence.

It was around that time that Thomas had asked me to step up as the new Sheriff in town and protect Collier Pack. How could I say no to my Alpha and one of my very best friends?

I couldn't.

The fact that Katherine had set boundaries I couldn't breach had only made it easier for me to say yes.

Still, we'd broken things off and, for a while, I'd tried to stay away and give her the space she wanted. But I can't. Lord knows I've tried, but I can't.

I need her like I need air to breathe, but she's only human and she doesn't feel the same about me. I don't know how to fix it and I have an entire Pack to protect, secrets that aren't fully mine to share.

I could never put my Pack or my Alpha in danger. It was my job to shelter them from the human world, not invite humans into it.

I knew in my heart that I would never take a mate. Katherine was mine even if I couldn't claim her as such. This was simply the life I was meant to live, and I'd made peace with that and was doing the best I could with the cards I'd been dealt.

My phone rang and I scowled.

Now what?

"Sheriff Blakely."

"Quick, 9-1-1. We have an emergency."

Recognizing the voice, my heart plummeted into my stomach.

"Winnie? Is that you? What's happened?"

"No one told me today was Clay's birthday."

I groaned.

"That's it? You just called in an emergency for Clay's birthday?"

"Yes. Now drop whatever you're doing and get your sexy little ass over here right now. He'll be home at five and if I'm going to surprise him, I need all of you here. I already talked to Cruz and Brady on account they're working with him today and they're going to stall for a few extra minutes, but it's important to have all his boys here to help celebrate."

I chuckled. "Clay will hate this plan."

"No he won't. He was just complaining how the six of you haven't gotten together in a hot minute. Now move it. We're running out of time."

I shook my head and looked around at the files on my desk. They could wait another day. This was Clay, after all. Heck, there was nothing I wouldn't do for any of the Six Pack. They were my closest and best friends since childhood, and we always stuck together through thick or thin.

"I'm on my way," I told her.

"Yes! Thank you. You're the best. I owe you."

"And I'm going to remind you of that often."

She was still laughing as she disconnected the call.

I gathered my stuff and locked up my office for the night.

"Heading out early, sir?" Deaton asked.

"Apparently Clay's birthday now constitutes as a Pack emergency," I explained with a chuckle.

"It's been a slow day around here anyway," he said.

I knew a passive aggressive statement when I heard one. "Draw straws for who carries the emergency phone this evening. Ryder will be on call tonight and through the weekend starting at ten. Be available for any emergencies until then and otherwise enjoy your weekend."

"Thanks boss," they both told me as I fled the building.

I had already gotten Clay's present weeks ago but wasn't expecting to see him today.

On my way home to grab it, I called Thomas.

"Yes, I'm coming," he answered.

I laughed. "Winnie already got to you, huh?"

"Yes. We're wrangling the girls to drop them off at Peyton's and then we'll be on our way. Trust me, five o'clock, I know."

"She is quite persuasive."

"She definitely is that," he agreed. "We have to swing by the barn and grab Opal so he doesn't get too suspicious if Ruby bails early since she's the one on call this weekend, or something like that."

"You probably just got suckered."

He sighed. "You're probably right. Are you able to get away?"

"Yup. It's pretty quiet here and paperwork can wait until Monday. Besides, she did call it a 9-1-1 emergency."

"She didn't."

"Oh she did."

"That's hysterical."

"Thomas! Come on, we're going to be late," his mate called in the background.

"Gotta run. See you in a little bit."

"Good luck."

I pulled up to my house and jumped out to dash inside and grab Clay's gift. The lady at the store even wrapped it for me. I wasn't sure that was something they normally did for free or not, but

I asked nicely and winked at her. She'd readily agreed and even gave me her phone number.

I had that effect on females, whether shifters or human, it never seemed to matter. I tried not to abuse it too much, but I wasn't above using it to my advantage. Though knowing I wasn't going to even date anytime soon, if ever, I should probably feel a little guilty about it, but I didn't.

Back in the car, I sped over to Winnie and Clay's place just as the others were starting to arrive too.

Winnie ran outside waving her arms in the air.

"You guys can't park here, or he'll know."

I groaned. This was turning out to be a pain in my ass.

"Come on, you guys can park at the diner, and we can run over together," Wyatt offered, though I noticed his mate, Kate jumped out and went inside to help Winnie instead.

The rest of us drove over to the diner.

I wasn't looking forward to stripping and carrying my clothes to run back. At the last minute, Thomas drove by and slowed to a stop when he saw us.

"What are you doing? Aren't we supposed to be meeting at Clay's?" he asked.

I rolled my eyes. "Winnie doesn't want all the vehicles there when he gets home."

"I told you," Lily said.

"Fine, we'll park here too."

"Or you could just give us all a lift and park in the abandoned barn back behind his house," I suggested. "Not enough room for all of us but one truck will fit."

"Good idea. I like how you think," Lily said, impressed. "Hop in the back and we'll drive everyone over."

Wyatt, Austin, Emmett, and I jumped into the back and rode back to Clay's place. It felt like old times already having my boys all together riding in a truck out into the fields after we dropped Lily off at the house.

By the time we made it back, Winnie was on edge and a nervous wreck. Bran and Ruby were there already too.

Ruby is one of Thomas's sisters and she and Clay are close friends, as they share management responsibilities at the dairy barn where he works.

Living in a large wolf shifter pack meant everyone pitched in for the good of the Pack. I'd certainly taken on responsibilities that I wasn't overly fond of. We all did what we had to do.

Thomas became our current Alpha after his father stepped down several years ago. Zach had been a fair and strong Alpha, but my loyalty to Thomas went far beyond Pack obligations.

The Six Pack are my chosen family. Not that I didn't have a good relationship with my own family, but I wasn't nearly as close to them as I am to the guys.

For as long as I could remember it was the Six Pack taking on the world. Shortly after high school Wyatt met Austin's cousin Kate, his true mate. Their mating period had been a long one which is practically unheard of for true mates, but we were so young, and they had things they needed or at least wanted to do before officially settling down.

In truth, they'd spent every single day together, so I didn't really understand why it mattered if they were mated or not.

Next came Thomas. We'd all sat back and enjoyed the show as his stubborn, opinionated, unfiltered mate blew in like a tornado and turned his life upside down. They took over as Alpha and Pack Mother soon after and were popping out daughters like crazy.

We all teased him frequently about being unable to give us a proper male heir. Then again, he had six older sisters, so maybe it was genetic or something.

I'd found my Katherine around the same time, but as there were significant issues with her being human and I was a shifter, I'd kept her to myself. It was the one thing in my life I'd never shared with the guys, and I likely never would.

I knew it wasn't healthy for me to think of her as *my* anything, but I couldn't help it. She would always be mine, and quite frankly, I did a lot of unhealthy things when it came to Katherine Carter.

Clay on the other hand was probably the most levelheaded of all of us but he hadn't handled mating Winnie well. I think we were all happy to have that behind us now.

Austin and Emmett remained blissfully happy bachelors.

"They're on their way. Everyone in place," Winnie shouted.

The place looked like a party store puked all over it. There were streamers and balloons everywhere. Clay was going to positively hate it, yet because it's important to his mate, he'd love it too.

Being the center of attention was never his favorite place to be. I was happy to see she only kept it to his core friends, those of us that truly meant something to him. He'd be okay with this, maybe even happy since he was always harping on us to get together.

In truth, I missed the easy days of just hanging out with my best friends without a care in the world.

"He's here," Lily whisper-yelled at us.

We all kept quiet, as if he couldn't hear nearly a dozen hearts beating in his house. We were shifters after all. It wasn't like our accelerated hearing made it easy for surprises.

"Come on, Clay. Just let us come in for a little bit. I'm starving and Winnie always makes the best dinners," Cruz whined.

"Go to Kate's if you're that hard up for a hot meal," Clay grumbled.

"I'm not saying there's anything wrong with Kate's, but I live with Peyton who does a lot of the cooking there. Which means it's all I ever eat. Winnie's cooking is a real treat."

It wasn't true and we all knew it, but they were doing a fantastic job of distracting him as he walked in.

"Surprise!" we all yelled as he stumbled backwards in obvious surprise.

"Happy birthday, Clay," I shouted.

He groaned and shook his head.

"Whose idea was this?"

We all pointed to Winnie as a wide smile crossed his face. He swooped her up in his arms and kissed her hard and unashamedly.

How I envied him.

Katherine
Chapter 2

Dinner with my parents had been a disaster. Everything was fine right up until dad mentioned *him*.

"Had a new case cross my desk this morning. A couple of Collier kids stirring up some trouble in town. I imagine James will be around to help clear it up."

"James?" Mom had asked. "Katherine's James?"

"The one and only."

"I always did like that boy."

"Why exactly did you break up with him, Katherine?"

I groaned just thinking back on it and I couldn't eat fast enough to get out of there.

James Blakely, the one I let get away, or at least that's what everyone in my family seemed to think.

In truth, we had been young and the intensity of my feelings for him had scared the life out of me. I regretted letting him go, though. He'd wanted a commitment, like the happily ever after kind, and it had made my head swim.

I'd tried to date since then and no one ever seemed to make the cut.

No one else was *him*.

He was the mark of which I measured all men to and everyone else fell significantly short.

Sometimes I wondered if I sucked it up and went to him if he would still take me back, but my ego wouldn't let me try. Instead, every time I was in the same room with him, the tension between us put me on edge and I said and did things I didn't mean, or when possible, I just panicked and walked away.

I knew it was just a defense mechanism. We'd only dated for a short time and that had been years ago, yet my body still craved him. He still haunted my every dream and was the star of all my fantasies.

I got hot and wet just hearing his name and all it did was piss me off.

"Can we please just have dinner without talking about him?"

"We just worry about you, sweetie. You don't date. Work consumes you. There's more to life, Katherine."

I huffed, ready to pack up leftovers and get the hell out of there.

"I know, Mom. But I'm happy with my life, really."

It wasn't entirely a lie. I loved helping children in the community. They meant a lot to me and in some cases I was the only advocate they'd ever have.

"Will I be seeing you in my court room next week?"

"I don't think so. The case hasn't been brought to my attention," I told him honestly.

He smiled slyly. "I don't know any cases involving minors that you don't manage to get your hands on."

"Fine, I'll bite. What's the case?"

"Three Collier minors got kicked out of the movie theater and then vandalized the building in anger."

"Vandalized how?"

Mom smacked his arm and scowled at him.

"This wasn't vandalism, and you know it. You shouldn't even be taking the case. Colliers will handle it themselves. They always do," she reminded him.

"But this wasn't in town and there's a new cop in town that's got the DA all riled up over it."

"How did they vandalize the building?" I asked again.

Dad sighed. "Water balloons."

"Seriously? That's it?"

"That's it."

"Did they at least leave the balloon mess behind?"

"Nope. They cleaned it all up."

I glared at him. "I'm with Mom. Why are you even accepting this case?"

"The new guy added public misconduct to the case. Probably after Bucky told him destruction of property wasn't going to hold."

"Well, a public misconduct charge should come across the desk soon. I'll take a look at it, but it sounds pretty cut and dry here."

"Maybe you should get in there and investigate what's going on over there."

I snorted. "Dad, Elizabeth will never let that happen and you know it. Heck, even when I dated James, Collier property lines were off limits."

Mom frowned. "You've never been there?"

"No more than a drive through town or an uncomfortable attempt to eat at the tavern. Not something I'd put on my to-do list again. They're a strange bunch. Call it paranoid or protective or whatever. They don't like outsiders and go out of their way to make you feel uncomfortable if you dare go there."

"But they're so nice. I was just talking to Peyton at Powell's Grocery, and she was telling me all about the greenhouse her brothers-in-law were building behind her house. They have a full hydroponics system up and running at Kate's Diner too. It's so fascinating."

"And when the Larken Trailer Park burned down a few years back, they all up and moved into Collier territory. They didn't seem to have any issues with that."

"I don't know what to tell you guys. Maybe it's just me they don't like then."

"Oh, Katherine. Don't be so dramatic."

"Why are we even talking about the Colliers?"

"Because of the case," Dad reminded me, but there was a mischievous spark in his eyes that told me it was far more than that.

"Okay, well, I love you both and thanks for dinner, but I'm exhausted and ready to settle in for the night. Can I help with dishes?"

"I've got it," Dad said. "You go get some rest."

I got up with a smile and kissed his cheek then hugged Mom goodbye.

My dad was one of the good guys. While Mom had stayed home since I was born, took care of the house, and managed his life, every night Dad was home for dinner and cleaned up afterward.

Those simple gestures were a love language all their own and something I longed for in a man.

I didn't mind cooking or cleaning up afterwards but give me a man who would do the laundry and I'd marry him in a heartbeat.

The drive home was mostly uneventful, but as I pulled up to my house there was a car parked out front that I didn't recognize.

I lived in the woods on a dirt road. I liked the solitude. James had liked it too and had helped me pick it out when we were still dating.

Brushing that thought from my mind, I grabbed my handgun from the glove compartment and put it in my coat pocket and then fisted the pepper spray on my keychain as I got out of the car. A single girl in this world couldn't be cautious enough.

"Who's there?" I yelled out.

The door to the dark sedan opened and Allen stepped out.

Tension began to subside, but only a little. It was late and as far as I could remember he had no reason to be here. Plus, it was as if something was missing.

I stopped and listened to the surroundings. I could still hear the sounds of the night, but I was certain something was off.

My usual sense of peace was replaced with anxiety. I couldn't really explain it.

"Allen? What are you doing here?"

"Hi. Sorry to startle you. New car. Do you like it?"

"Uh, yeah, sure."

"I was getting worried. You're usually home by now and you weren't answering your phone."

I looked down at where I'd already dialed 911 ready to call them before I realized it was just him. I found the phone was still on do not disturb from an earlier meeting I had.

"Sorry. All fixed. I forgot to take it off do not disturb."

"Where were you?"

I didn't know why he thought that was any of his business, but I answered him anyway.

"My parents' for dinner."

"Oh, yeah, I didn't think to look there," he muttered to himself.

"Allen, is there something you need?"

"Uh, well, a new case came in today and I wanted to make sure you saw it."

Allen worked with me. He was relatively new to the area and seemed to just attach himself to me. Half the office thought we were dating. I'd agreed to dinner with him once. It wasn't terrible, but I knew without a doubt he just wasn't the one for me.

He wasn't James, I thought with a sigh.

Normally I kept my obsession with the sexy Sheriff of Collier under wraps. I supposed with my parents' insistence on talking about him tonight that it was bound to have escaped the careful little box I crammed those emotions into, as I did once again.

"Is there something that needs to be addressed tonight?" I asked him suddenly worried I'd missed something important for not turning my phone back on sooner.

"Uh, no. It can wait."

"Oh, so why are you here then?"

He sighed. "Fine, you caught me. I haven't seen you much and I miss you."

"Allen, we see each other every day in the office."

"I know. I meant outside of work. I don't really have a lot of friends in the area, and I get lonely."

And that was how he'd convinced me to go out with him that one time.

"Look, I don't think that's such a…"

"Just as friends," he insisted. "Please? Tomorrow night? You're not doing anything this weekend are you? There wasn't anything on your calendar at the office."

"You went through my desk at the office?"

He shrugged sheepishly.

"Allen, you can't do that."

"I know, but will you? Just dinner?"

"Fine," I conceded even though I didn't want to. Anything to get him to leave so I could crash for the night.

There wasn't exactly much excitement in my life these days to spend Friday night with my parents. It wouldn't hurt me to go out once in a while.

Allen stepped closer to me, and I started to get uncomfortable. That should have been a red flag enough to bail on him for another date, but mostly he was a sweet guy, and I didn't know how to get out of it. I didn't exactly have a ton of experience with the opposite sex. James had been the only man I'd ever seriously dated.

"Look, it's late, and I'm tired. I'll see you tomorrow."

"I'll pick you up at six," Allen said.

"How about if I just meet you somewhere?"

"Nah, I got this."

He was entirely clueless to the fact that I was uncomfortable with this situation.

I wasn't sure what exactly changed, but I was suddenly at ease and that feeling of sanctuary I got from my house made me shudder. It somehow also gave me courage.

"Allen, I'll meet you. Where are we going?"

He closed the gap between us right into my personal space and reached out to take my hand.

"Relax, Katherine, I said I'd pick you up here."

Suddenly there was a growl from somewhere nearby that caused Allen to stumble off the porch. I could have saved him, but instead, I pulled my hand back at the last second.

There was another growl. I should have been terrified, but I wasn't. There was something almost comforting about it. And I held back a laugh trying to escape as Allen ran for his car.

"Call animal control. What the hell was that?" he yelled through a cracked window in the safety of his car while I stood there on my porch entirely unaffected.

"Look around you, Allen. We're out in the country. I'm not calling Animal Control for a piece of nature. I choose to just live in peace with the animals here. He won't hurt me," I told him with certainty.

If anything, the dog or wolf, or whatever it was, more likely had been trying to protect me from Allen and for that I was grateful.

That seemed like an odd thing to think about a wild beast, but I couldn't bring myself to be scared of it.

"Katherine, please. At least get inside the house so I know you're safe."

"I'm fine," I told him, but if it meant he'd leave, I was all for it. "Thanks," I whispered into the night, not for Allen, but to whatever beast had just scared the life out of him.

James

Chapter 3

The party had lasted a lot longer than I'd anticipated, but it was great to catch up with the guys. I missed them when we didn't get together often enough, but I was just as much to blame for that.

As soon as I left Clay and Winnie's house, I drove home and parked. I didn't even go into the house. I just stripped and left my clothes on the front porch and then I shifted to make the six point three miles run to Katherine's house.

Lately I couldn't even remember the last time I'd slept in my own bed. I probably spent more time in my fur than any other wolf in Collier Pack. I couldn't help myself.

For a few years I'd managed to stay away from her, but I always kept tabs on my woman. About a month ago a new male had moved to town. It hadn't taken much to find out he was working with Katherine. I didn't like that, but when I'd discovered she'd gone out on a date with him, my obsession had flared worse than ever.

I was usually settled into the little den I'd made for myself under her front porch earlier. Tonight, I was late because of the party. When I arrived, he was there. I could smell him before I even reached the house and he set my wolf on edge.

If Katherine got serious about this guy, I didn't know what I was going to do. At some point I knew I was going to have to confide in Thomas and ask him to either sedate me, command me to forget her, or restrain me from going after him.

The sad truth was that I didn't think any of those methods would even work. My draw to her was as strong as any mating call I'd ever heard of.

Mine, my wolf growled in my head.

We were certainly in agreement there.

I snuck around the corner and ducked under the deck when I saw they were standing on the front steps talking.

The fear and stress I'd smelled rolling off her as I'd approached seemed to suddenly disappear. I wasn't sure what had changed, but she was no longer afraid. Still, I could sense she was uneasy and when that asshole took her hand all I could see was red.

It took everything in my power not to burst out of my hiding spot and rip his throat out.

How dare he touch my mate!

A deep guttural growl rumbled through me as I started to hone in on my prey.

The guy stumbled off the porch and ran for his car.

I couldn't hear what they were saying over the roaring in my ears.

But Katherine turned to walk back inside.

"Thanks," I clearly heard her whisper.

My wolf settled, somehow knowing that was meant for us.

The idiot who'd almost lost his life tonight drove off without any further interactions.

A few moments later, the front door opened again. I could smell steak that made my mouth water.

She walked down the steps and around the corner to where there was no lattice covering the side of the porch and she set down a large steak and a bowl of water.

I lifted my head and knew the moment she caught sight of me.

She gasped, then smiled.

"Thanks for having my back. He'll be back tomorrow around six o'clock if you happen to be around. I may need an assist. He doesn't seem to take no for an answer very well."

Suddenly her shoulders sagged, and she frowned.

"My life has been reduced to talking to a wild wolf. I'm an idiot. I should be calling Animal Control to handle this, not feeding him."

She sighed, then shook her head.

"I know you can't understand me, but I'm not afraid of you. I appreciate what you did tonight. I hope you're comfortable enough under there. Sweet dreams, my wolf."

She walked away leaving me stunned.

She knew I was here.

She wasn't afraid of me.

My heart lightened, yet I couldn't let myself hope for even a second that she could actually feel this bond between us. She was only human after all.

With Katherine safely in her house, I happily ate the steak and lapped up the water before settling down for the night.

Nothing would stop me from being there.

Six o'clock. It was a date.

I settled down and slept more soundly than I had in a long time.

*****

The next morning, I awoke early and ran back home. It was Saturday so I didn't have much on my plate, but I wasn't dumb enough to hang around during the day. That was just asking to be shot by some well-meaning do-gooder.

Running roughly twelve and a half miles a day in my fur was keeping my wolf strong. It also seemed to make me hungry.

Once home I grabbed my clothes off the porch and let myself in. I went straight for the shower, then changed and called Thomas.

"Hey," he answered knowing it was just me.

"Breakfast?"

"Kate's in twenty?"

"Perfect. I'm starving."

I wanted to talk this madness over with him, but I couldn't. Katherine was my burden to bear. We weren't even on speaking terms anyway so there was no reason to drag him into this. Still, I needed to talk to someone to know I wasn't going completely insane.

I was positive Katherine was human, but I also knew in my heart that she was my one true mate. I'd always known it. I just couldn't bring myself to accept it—until now.

All these years I'd been able to control it. As long as I was near her a few times a week, it was enough. But seeing her with that asshole had certainly stirred something within me that I couldn't shake now.

Already the only thing I wanted to do was turn back and camp out on her doorstep just to be close enough to hear the beating of her heart.

I was fairly certain she didn't entirely like this guy, though it sounded like she was going on another date with him tonight anyway. That bothered me a lot.

How much worse would it get if she actually fell in love with another man?

I physically shook as fur sprouted across the tops of my hands just thinking about it.

This was getting bad.

Pulling up to Kate's, I didn't dare get out of my truck as I sat there taking deep breaths and trying to calm myself down.

I couldn't exactly walk inside like this. It would only spur a million questions and a whole lot of gossip.

I had no idea how long I sat there, but I jumped at the sound of someone knocking on my window.

Thomas's eyes widened when I turned to see who was there.

He motioned for me to roll the window down, which I did. Something in his eyes told me this was my Alpha Thomas, not my friend.

"Calm yourself," he said as I felt the tingling sensation of his Alpha powers wash over me.

My wolf instantly submitted, but it still left me shaken.

He walked around the front of my vehicle without a word and then opened the door and climbed inside.

"Drive," he ordered.

"Where?" I asked.

"Don't care. Just drive."

I nodded and did as he commanded.

We were both quiet for a while. I could feel him watching me as I took the backroads keeping within Pack territory lines.

"Are you okay?" he finally asked.

"Yeah. I'm fine," I lied.

He'd seen me, the desperate parts of me that I was barely holding together. That wasn't something he was just going to forget about.

"Who is she?" he asked.

"What? Who?"

How could he possibly know.

"Well, you're not injured that I can see. No blood that I can smell. So there's only one reason I know of for a male to get that worked up and that's his true mate."

"She's not my true mate," I said, tasting the lie on my tongue.

He gave me a knowing look but didn't argue.

"Are you even aware that you sat there for over twenty minutes unable to calm your wolf?"

"You counted?"

"Yeah, I was watching to see what you'd do until I couldn't stand to see you like that a second longer."

I smacked the steering wheel in frustration.

"I didn't want you to see me like that."

"I know, but I wasn't going to just sit there and let you continue to suffer like that."

I sighed. "I'm fine, Thomas. I'm handling it."

"Who is she?"

"No one you know," I lied.

Kids from Collier, especially since the Larken wolves joined our Pack, caused trouble in town enough times that he was plenty familiar and used to dealing with Katherine Carter.

"You are aware I can smell when you're lying."

I scoffed. "You can't smell a lie, Thomas."

"I can. It's an Alpha thing."

"Bullshit."

He chuckled. "Fine, I can't smell it, but I do know. And I don't have to use any Alpha traits to know either, because I know *you*, James."

"Whatever."

"Look, I know how crazy everything feels going through this. I've been there, remember? I'm mated to Lily, your Pack Mother, the woman who called me the biggest douchebag on the planet and ran home with her tail between her legs the second she started to feel anything."

"That was your mate?"

"Smartass. I'm just saying that I get it."

"Thomas, there's nothing to get."

"Now it's my turn to call bullshit."

"Please, just stay out of this."

"No."

"Thomas."

"No, James. I will not stay out of this. I will not forget about it. And I really hope you don't make me command you to tell me.

27

I'm your oldest friend, and I'm here for you, no matter what. You can talk to me."

I sighed. "You won't understand."

"I will."

"Not this time."

"Try me."

"She's not like us," I blurted out.

He didn't respond immediately as he chewed it over.

"Okay, that's not the norm, but it's still possible. Chase Westin and his mate, Jenna, aren't exactly normal, but they are true mates. His mother has a saying that God never makes a mistake when pairing mates, or something like that. It's a little unorthodox, but they make it work. I'm not some archaic asshole of an Alpha, you know. So what is she?"

I shook my head.

"Come on. Are you going to make me guess? Is she a fox? Or how about a skunk? Wait, I know, is she an elephant?"

"Human. She's human."

He went silent and when I looked over his mouth was gaped open and there was a look of concentration on his face.

"Katherine?" he finally asked.

"What? Come on."

I tried to protest but couldn't form the words to all out deny it.

"I mean, it makes sense."

"What makes sense about that?"

He shot me a knowing look.

"James, she's the only woman you've ever shown any interest in. How long have you known she's your true mate?"

I sighed. There was no sense in trying to deny it now.

"Since the first moment I laid eyes on her."

"But that was years ago."

"I'm aware."

"But…" I could tell he was thinking back through everything. "But you haven't been like this all that time."

"I know. I've been handling it. As long as I'm near her regularly, it's tolerable."

"Near her? I thought you avoided her like the plague."

"In my skin, yeah."

"She's met your wolf?"

I shrugged thinking back to just last night when she'd seen me under her porch in the moonlight.

"Are you insane?"

"Probably."

"How often do you go over there?'

"Every night I'm not on call," I admitted. "I have a den under her porch where I sleep."

"Wow. I need a minute to let that sink in." He sat there, trying to process it all as I pulled up to a spot near the river that we used to hang out at and drink beer as teenagers. "So, what changed?"

"Huh?"

"What changed? If you've been secretly doing this for years, then something had to have changed, because I've never seen you like this before."

"I'll be fine."

"What changed, James?"

I sighed. "She's dating someone."

"Shit."

"Yeah."

We sat there in silence, each lost in our own thoughts.

Finally, I cracked. He already knew enough at this point; I might as well just dive in with the rest.

"I'm not sure she actually likes him, but it just got me to thinking, what if she falls in love with some asshole? Then what? She lives happily ever after while I'm just stuck in limbo like this?"

He growled. "I can't let that happen to you. I've already lived it with my sister."

"It's not the same."

"It's exactly the same."

"It's not. I remember how Lizzy was during that time in her life. It's not that bad. I promise. Maybe because she's human and doesn't feel the bond the same as I do, but I am okay. I just got in my head and freaked out a little."

"A little?"

"Fine, a lot, but I am handling it."

Thomas's oldest sister had suffered for years with an unresolved bond. It had nearly killed her, and she walked around like a shell of herself. It was scary, but that wasn't me. I wasn't numb to life, at least not yet. I understood why he would be so concerned, though.

"What are you going to do?"

"Nothing."

"What? If she's really your true mate…"

"Thomas, she's human. She can never know about me. I was ready to leave the Pack and run away with her once upon a time, but I'm older now and I have responsibilities and people who rely on me. I can't be selfish about this, and I can't risk the safety of the Pack to try and explain things to her."

"But…"

"No. I appreciate that, but no. It won't work and I won't selfishly put everyone else's life in danger like that. I swore an oath to protect them, to protect you, and that's just as important to me."

"But…"

"I'm not going to change my mind, so don't even waste your breath."

"Will you just shut up and let me speak already. There have been cases of shifters mating humans. It can happen. There have been rumors of human shifter true mate bonds. I get it won't be easy, but it is possible. From what I know about it, she won't feel the bond as strongly as you, but she will feel it."

"She hates me, man. It'll never work."

He sat there and laughed.

I growled in frustration.

"You know, love and hate are opposite sides of the emotional coin, yet often one is mistaken for the other. Think about it. The feelings aren't so different and equally strong."

"You're insane. There's a huge difference between hate and love."

"Is there?"

Hours later I was still contemplating his theory as I ran to Katherine's house. As I snuck under the porch, I stopped in my tracks. In the hole of my little den was a freaking dog bed.

I shook my head, smiling to myself, as I settled in, praying I wouldn't do anything stupid.

Katherine

Chapter 4

I was anxious and just wanted to call Allen and cancel our dinner plans when I looked up and saw the wolf running across the yard.

This eerie calm sort of washed over me.

I gave it a minute, trying to pull myself together, and then grabbed the new water and food bowls I'd bought for him today. I had already put the bedding down and hoped maybe it would be a little more comfortable than the ground.

It was probably stupid. He was a freaking wild animal, a wolf. I was certain I'd lost my mind, yet I wasn't scared of him. He made me feel safe, as if he were standing watch over me. It was as if I knew, without a doubt, that he would protect me against absolutely anything.

Of course, I had no way of knowing for sure, and certainly had no desire to try and test the theory, but I felt so sure of it.

In truth, I was relieved he'd come back before Allen arrived. It felt like everything was going to be okay now.

I walked outside with a fresh bowl of water and the other bowl filled with leftover casserole I was going to throw out. For some reason my last second shopping spree had stopped just short of buying him dogfood. Did wolves even eat dogfood? I didn't know for sure, and I didn't want to offend him.

I laughed to myself as I set the food down.

It sounded like I was making him out to be a real person or something and not just a beast that any sane person would be terrified of.

"I'm glad you made it back before Allen arrived. Allen, that's his name. We work together and well, he's new in town and sort of guilted me into a date. This is our second, but there's absolutely no chemistry there. I should have said no, and I don't even know why I didn't, probably to just diffuse the situation and get away from him in the moment."

I stopped and frowned as I dared to look under the porch to find the large wolf curled up on the bed with his head cocked to the side as if he was listening and could actually understand what I was saying.

I laughed to myself and shook my head.

"I know you can't understand me, but thanks for listening anyway. So here's the plan. I'm going to go to dinner because I hate letting people down and I did promise, even though it wasn't like he gave me much of a choice."

I growled a little just thinking about it. Then I sighed. What was done was done. I would just try to make the most of it and call it as early a night as I could get away.

"I didn't want him to pick me up so I wouldn't be stuck all night, but he's quite persistent. I do not want him coming inside though, so if things get out of hand, please feel free to step in again like you did last night."

The sound of a car across the gravel alerted me to his early arrival.

"Of course he's early," I muttered. "Stay warm tonight. Hopefully I won't be gone long."

I peeked out from under the porch and then ran around to the back of the house and let myself in. I didn't want to alert Allen to the wolf's presence again. He'd already threatened to call Animal Control on him, not that I would ever allow that to happen.

I couldn't really explain why I was so protective of this creature, but as long as he didn't bother me, I wasn't going to bother him. And I sure as hell wasn't going to allow anyone else to hurt him.

Allen seemed to take forever to park and come to the door. I didn't want to just rush outside and seem anxious, but I was also ready to just get this date over with.

At last, he finally knocked. I grabbed my purse rushed out of the door nearly plowing into him.

"Hi," he said, startled. "Are we in a rush?"

"Just hungry."

"Oh, well, I guess we can head over and see if we can get a table earlier. I made a reservation for seven."

I looked down at my watch noting it was only six.

What the hell was he expecting to do for an hour?

"Oh, okay, so what do you want to do for an hour then?"

A whole bloody hour before even getting to dinner?

This was putting me in a foul mood right off the bat.

"I thought maybe you'd invite me in and we'd see where the night leads."

"Yup, not going to happen. I have a no men policy here. Haven't had the best experiences in the past."

"Oh. I'm sorry. I didn't know."

"Why should you?"

"Okay, then," he said clearly rethinking his plans for the night. "Well, we can drive over and see how busy they are, I guess. Maybe they can fit us in early."

"Sure. Sounds great. Where are we going?"

"This place called Collier Steakhouse and Tavern. It's a little ways away but has great reviews. Have you been there?"

"Uh, that's in Collier County."

"Yes, but it's not far," he insisted.

"No, but they don't exactly like outsiders. It's kind of hard to explain. I'm sure the food is great, but they'll go out of their way to make you feel unwelcome there."

"What? No way. Reviews say the service is great there, best place around actually."

I groaned. "You have a lot to learn about things around here. Collier County is considered cult-like territory to most. It's best if we just stay clear of that."

He looked disappointed, but there was no way I was setting a foot inside Collier, not even so much as my little pinky toe. It wasn't happening.

"You really don't want to go there, do you?"

"No," I said frankly.

Allen sighed in frustration. "Fine. Let's see how long the line to Simmons is. The reviews there were nowhere as good but seemed decent enough."

"Simmons is great," I tried to assure him.

Not only was I telling the truth about Collier, they are closed off, snobbish, and make anyone that doesn't live there feel bad for intruding, but it also put me at risk of running into James and that was something I wanted to avoid at all costs, especially with Allen in tow.

Even when we were dating, he never took me to places in Collier. That more than affirmed all the rumors I knew of the place, at least to me.

He helped me to the car and held the door open for me. We chatted lightly about nothing of any relevance as we drove into town.

The restaurant was bustling, a popular date night destination.

Allen slipped the hostess some money to move us up the list and it worked. We were seated quickly though I was stopped a few times by well-meaning acquaintances curiously watching me and Allen.

I didn't exactly live in a big bustling city. Everyone seemed to know everyone around here, or at least it often felt that way.

Worse, everyone was always up in everyone else's business. I had no doubt that coming here meant word would get back to my parents quickly.

Maybe risking going into Collier wouldn't have been the worst idea.

Too late to turn back now.

I tried to stay focused on what he was saying but I could also feel eyes on us, which was a little unsettling. I doubt it would have bothered me if he were someone I wouldn't mind being connected to outside of the office, but poor Allen, he would never be more than a coworker to me. I just didn't think he knew that, yet.

"So, Katherine, you were raised around here, right?" he asked just as the waitress approached us.

"Hi, I'm Paula and will be serving you tonight. What can I get you two to drink?"

"Two glasses of your finest wine," Allen answered for us.

I gritted my teeth. I hated when guys did that. He'd done it the last time too which had been a huge red flag for me that things were never going to work out between us.

"And a glass of water," I added defiantly.

"You got it. Can I get you started with an appetizer or something?"

"We'll need a minute to look over the menu," he was quick to reply.

"Actually, I'm ready if you know what you want," I said sweetly.

"Oh, well, okay then. I'll have the ribeye, well done, the broccoli, no salt or butter, and plain brown rice."

"Um, the rice is pilaf and already has vegetables and stuff in it. I'm not sure it's actual brown rice, but I can check."

He sighed in frustration. "Just make it the rice pilaf if you must."

Wow. Boring and flavorless.

"Would you like me to order for you?" he asked.

"No thanks. I've got it. I'll also have the ribeye, rare."

"That's with a cool red center?"

"The bloodier the better," I assured her, taking slight pleasure in watching Allen cringe a little. "Baked potato, fully loaded, and the roasted Brussel sprouts."

"You've got it," she said taking our menus.

"That's a high sodium meal you just ordered. That cannot be good for your blood pressure," he commented.

I just smiled. "No blood pressure concerns here. I'm healthy as an ox."

"Mm-hmm," he said not sounding convinced.

"So, you were saying?" I asked suddenly ready to get through this night in record time.

"Oh, yes, you grew up around here, right?"

"Born and raised. I went away for a few years for college and couldn't return fast enough. I wouldn't want to live anywhere else."

His brow furrowed. "There's little to do around here though. Doesn't it get boring?"

I laughed. "No. Not for me. I don't need much and I'm not big on night life and stuff like that."

"I see."

"Before moving here, what did you like to do in your free time?"

"Well, on the weekends I'd usually be out clubbing with friends. I haven't found anything even close to a nightclub within driving distance of this place."

"Yeah, closest you'll get around here is the BBQ joint down the street. They have country line dancing on Thursdays."

He shook his head. "That's not even close to the same."

I genuinely laughed at the look of disgust on his face.

"Allen, you moved to the country, in literally the middle of nowhere. You are hours away from the closest city. What did you really expect?"

"I don't know. Some signs of modern civilization. Is that really too much to ask?"

"For around here? Yes."

"It's certainly been a culture shock."

"I imagine so. I'd probably be a complete fish out of water trying to live in a big city. I don't even enjoy visiting them."

"What? No way. You have to let me take you and show you what you're missing out on."

"Hard pass. I have no desire whatsoever. I love it here."

"You don't want to travel and see the world?"

"Nope."

"But everyone dreams of spreading their wings and experiencing new places."

"Not me."

He looked at me like I had two heads and I was grateful that Paula swung back by to check on us.

"Food should be up shortly. Just holler if you need anything."

"Holler?" Allen whispered when she walked away. "Like what does she expect us to do? Yell out, 'Yo, Paula, more wine over here?' That's ridiculous."

I shrugged. "I guess if you want more that badly."

His glass was almost empty while mine sat untouched. He seemed to take notice of that fact and frowned.

"Do you not like the wine?"

I shrugged. "It's red."

"Well, yeah, it pairs well with steak on top of being the best they have in house."

I pursed my lips. "Red wine gives me migraines."

He sighed. "Of course it does," he mumbled.

True to Paula's words, she returned quickly with our meals and we both dove in with gusto. I knew for me; I was just grateful to have something to do besides talk to him. And I wasn't certain but thought just maybe Allen felt the same way.

On our first date, I'd smiled and done all the expected things of me. I'd answered his questions in ways I thought he'd expect. I'd drank the damn wine, but at least it had been white wine.

I really disliked wine. I was much more of a beer or bourbon kind of woman.

This time I wasn't going to pretend to be someone interested, because I wasn't, and that wasn't fair to him.

I wasn't exactly known to be accommodating like that anyway, so he might as well know it now.

It had been nice and exciting to have a new man in town, and I'd given him the benefit of the doubt and tried. It was painfully clear he wasn't going to make the cut. Apparently, he hadn't felt quite so certain because here we were.

This time I wasn't going to sugar-coat things for him. With any luck, this would be the last time Allen asked to see me outside of work. We didn't need to make things awkward or leave anything hanging up in the air. I did still have to work with the guy.

He cringed as I cut into my steak and took a big juicy bite. "How can you eat that thing?" he asked.

I laughed. "How can you eat that thing? You ruined that steak. It might as well be called beef jerky at this point."

I was trying to tease him and lighten the mood, but I could see quickly that it was just irritating him.

The rest of the evening felt strained, and I turned down his request to do anything else after dinner, so he drove me home instead with an odd smile on his face.

I didn't wait for him to get out as I jumped from the car thanking him for dinner, but he was fast and insisted on walking me to my door.

"I'm glad you had a good time tonight," he informed me as I wondered briefly if he was insane.

What on Earth had I done or said to make him think that had been enjoyable in the least?

"And I'd much rather spend time alone with you than go out, too."

He pressed me against my front door and kissed me before I even knew what was happening.

His lips were wet and sloppy, slipping and sliding across mine. His tongue jutted out hard trying to find my own.

I started to gag and push him away as panic rose inside me, but then he froze as a feral growl echoed through the night.

Slowly he turned, keeping his back to me for protection, but had obvious irritation in the set of his shoulders.

"What is it about your damn dog?" he asked and then stumbled backwards knocking me into the door as my head slammed into it.

"Ow."

The wolf barked and snapped his teeth menacingly at Allen.

"Holy shit! That's a wolf. Get inside and call the cops now."

Somehow, I managed to get out from behind him as the wolf stalked towards the steps.

He looked terrifying and I was in complete awe as a slow smile broke out across my face. I slowly walked towards the beast instead of away from it. A calming assurance washed through me.

"Katherine! Are you insane?" Allen yelled. "Get back here!"

But I shook my head and walked over to the wolf who only stalled for a second to give me a curious look as I moved to stand safely behind my protector.

"Katherine, get away from that thing. He could kill you."

"He won't hurt me, but you, I'm not so sure." I wasn't positive if I meant he would hurt me or the wolf would hurt him. Maybe both. "I think you should leave Allen. It would be best if we didn't see each other outside of work again. This isn't working for me."

"What? But I thought we were getting along well."

"I have no idea what gave you that impression. We have absolutely nothing in common and if you really stop and think about it, you'll agree."

"But I thought you liked me. You invited me back here early."

The wolf growled again at his insinuations.

"I asked you to take me home early to end this date not to extend it alone with you. I never said or did anything to allude to that."

"You're a bitch. A total tease."

The wolf snapped his large jaws again as I reached down to run my hand through his soft fur letting him know I was okay.

"You should go."

He shook his head wildly. "You're insane. You know that."

"Sure," I said, just grateful when he moved to leave.

I fisted my hand in the thick fur at the nape of the wolf's neck hoping he wouldn't fight me and try to go after Allen, though I couldn't deny a bit of satisfaction if he did.

"Oh, and Allen, just so we are clear here. I am not interested in a third date, so don't ask. I was polite about the first two, but I won't be again."

He shook his head and jumped into his car as he sped off.

I sighed and sat down on the porch.

The wolf stood there watching me curiously.

"Thanks for having my back again. I don't know what I would have done if you hadn't come to the rescue. He's a bit of an asshole."

I could have sworn the wolf raised his eyebrows at me as if saying, "Ya think?"

Did wolves even have eyebrows?

I snorted, amused by my thoughts.

"This is probably the signs of a nervous breakdown. I mean, I'm talking to a wolf. I should be terrified of you, but I'm not. So, do me a favor and don't do anything to change that. Stay my hero, wolf."

As if he somehow knew what I was talking about, he laid his big head in my lap and closed his eyes.

My breath caught, and then it was like a dam of emotions broke through as I wrapped my arms around his neck and gave into all the fear and frustration of the evening with Allen and cried.

James
Chapter 5

I hadn't seen Katherine in days, not since she'd wrapped her arms around me and cried. I'd hated not being able to hold her and tell her everything was going to be okay. It was comforting to know she trusted my wolf and sought refuge in him, but I knew if it had been me, the man version of me, she'd have put up a wall and run the other way.

As luck would have it, I was on call heading out of the weekend and into the week. Four freaking days in a row. The timing couldn't have been worse. I guess if I didn't have bad luck, I wouldn't have any luck at all.

It wasn't fair to my deputies that I was ill-tempered and miserable.

I hadn't seen my mate in days, and it was stressing me out that I didn't know if she was okay. It was hard not to allow the fears and paranoia to set in.

Was she okay?

Had that asshole returned?

Was she still upset?

I had a million questions running through my head and no answers. It wasn't like I could just pack up my cell phone and radio to sleep under her porch. If something had happened that required my immediate attention and I couldn't get there fast enough because I was a town away pining for a mate I would never truly have, I'd never forgive myself.

Still, despite my need to see her and know she is okay, I've been dreading this day for weeks. Not because I'm worried about what will happen in court today, but because I know she'll be there. Facing Katherine in person was very different than my time with her in my fur.

"All rise. The Honorable Judge George Carter presiding in the case of three minors vandalizing the local movie theater."

I scowled down at the three boys in question and nudged them forward to stand before the judge.

Both Thomas Collier and Luke Larken were in the courtroom.

With them here there was no reason why I needed to be. Sure, I'd passed the bar to fill in on minor cases like this, but it really wasn't my job, and this case wasn't in my jurisdiction.

"James. I haven't seen you in my courtroom in quite some time."

"I try not to make a habit of it, your honor."

The man's usual steel expression softened with just a hint of humor.

I didn't have to look around to know she wasn't there. It was a little surprising as normally she'd have her nose stuck into any case involving a child.

I didn't know the cop on the case, which was also surprising. I hadn't heard they were hiring and thought I knew everyone until this case came to my attention.

Judge Carter rubbed at his temple as he looked around the courtroom and shook his head.

"You're sure about this, Bucky?" he asked the District Attorney on the case.

"Yes sir. They were caught red-handed this time and we have it on video."

Mr. Terrence, the owner of the building in question was sitting next to him and leaned over to whisper something.

"You've got to be kidding me. Why?" Bucky said, loud enough for the entire room to hear.

I saw him look back towards Thomas and Luke and sigh.

"It was just a harmless prank. Kids being kids. I think they've learned their lesson. No need to take things any further."

"They defiled a building, sir. I have the footage on my patrol car camera even if Mr. Terrance decides to back out."

I shrugged and shot Bucky a smirk that was certain to irritate him. Half the battle in court with that fool was just keeping cool and letting him work himself up into a temper.

"Approach the bench, all three of you," he ordered.

I waited for Bucky and this new guy to approach before walking over to stand next to them.

"You're new around here, aren't you?"

"Yes sir. Just transferred in last month from Chicago."

Kudos to him for tossing around unfounded stature trying to look impressive. Too bad he had no clue how much Judge Carter hated a city boy.

"So, you're not exactly familiar with the dynamics of the area then. I just want to caution you to tread lightly. These are Collier boys and you do not want to piss off the Colliers."

"The law's the law, sir. We're prepared to defend this case, Colliers or not."

I refrained from shaking my head. This guy was just digging his own grave and making my job a whole lot easier.

"With all due respect, sir, there were no damages done. They threw water balloons at the building after being asked to leave for talking in the theater. And then they cleaned up the pieces when they were done venting. These aren't bad kids, sir, and this is clearly a waste of the court's time. They were charged with destruction of property yet there were no damages to report, and Mr. Terrance will attest to that."

The officer looked over at me curiously.

"Why are you even here? This isn't your jurisdiction," he challenged. "Yeah, I looked into you. I like to know who I'm going up against. You're Sheriff of Collier County."

"No, it isn't my jurisdiction, but if it concerns anyone who lives in Collier, you can be sure I'll be around. Besides, I'm not here as a Sheriff, but as their lawyer."

"No Elizabeth then?" the Judge asked, looking a little relieved.

"That's going to depend on how far he plans to take this. See at the time they were only charged with destruction of property. I'm prepared to prove there was no such destruction. Five days later, public misconduct was added on top of that."

"It's within my right after reviewing the film, sir."

"Yeah, I'm sure that's it," I muttered under my breath.

"That's enough, James."

"My apologies, sir."

"So, no Elizabeth then?" he asked again.

"I'll be filing a request for extension if this case proceeds. She's on her way."

"Well shit."

Bucky paled. "Elizabeth Collier? The Ice Queen?"

"The one and only," I assured him, not even bothering to point out she was Elizabeth Anderson now.

Elizabeth wasn't coming. She was tied up in San Marco at the moment. I knew that if I absolutely needed her, she would drop everything and come, but I was bluffing in hopes that just dropping her name would make them reconsider.

The door to the courtroom burst open and a tingle of awareness shot down my spine.

I braced myself for the punch that always came in her presence. As she approached the bench, I slowly turned to greet her.

"Hello, Katherine, so glad you could join us," I said sarcastically.

She glared at me as she took her place next to me at the bench.

"Sorry, I'm late, sir. What did I miss?"

"Mr. Terrence wants to drop the destruction of property charges, but your new hot-head here wants to proceed with public misconduct," I informed her.

"What are you doing here?" the arresting officer asked her.

"If it involves a minor in this court, you can be assured Child Protective Services will be involved," she said without even looking his way. "Judge, will this case be proceeding?"

"Go ahead and lay all the cards on the table so I know what I'm dealing with."

"There was no destruction of property," I insisted.

"Without Mr. Terrance's testimony, I don't have much of a case," Bucky insisted.

"This is insane. I still have video proof of destruction and public misconduct," the officer reminded him.

Bucky's face reddened. I was pretty certain he wasn't exactly thrilled being steamrolled like that. This guy certainly wasn't in the business of making friends.

"Ms. Carter, have you had time to look over the case?" her father asked.

"Not thoroughly sir. It just came to my attention."

"So what would you suggest then?"

"Delay for one week to allow me time to do a thorough child welfare check on the boys."

"These are Collier kids," I muttered. "It's not within your jurisdiction."

She shot me a look of warning. "With all due respect, your honor, that's the excuse given every time we encounter a delinquent matter out of Collier. The problem is, there is currently no CPS representative within that county, which poses a serious problem. Once this fact was brought to my office's attention, thank you Officer Dixon, I immediately filed for temporary liaison and was approved not even an hour ago. It is why I was late to your courtroom, your honor."

Dixon looked over at me with a knowing smirk, and then had the audacity to wink at me.

It took everything in my power not to punch him in the face as my hands fisted at my sides.

When Katherine went to hand her father the paperwork, I snatched it from her and looked it over for myself. Judge Hardwick had signed it only a few minutes earlier.

"Sonofabitch," I muttered under my breath.

Judge Carter watched me closely to see what I would do as he looked back and forth between me and Katherine.

"Look, I'm not trying to make trouble here. Two of the boys are first time offenders, but the other has crossed my desk more than once. I'm just saying it's worth a due diligence check."

"I'm going to assume that means you have everything in order," he said a little too gleefully. "In which case, I'm going to allow Ms. Carter's motion to delay. As I know Collier County isn't particularly fond of outsiders intruding on their territory, I will hold you personally accountable for her safety, James. Therefore, Katherine, you will check in with the Sheriff's office and be given an escort when in his jurisdiction. James, I'd consider it a personal favor if you would handle this situation personally and as discreetly as possible. It is not this court's wish to cause jurisdictional problems, but my judgement to proceed or dismiss will be largely based on Ms. Carter's findings."

He banged his gavel noting this as his final decision.

Bucky and Dixon grinned at each other as if this was some sort of victory. It wasn't. Nothing good could come from Katherine snooping around Collier territory, and absolutely no good would come from the two of us spending time together in our skin either.

I didn't wait around to chitchat or make plans. The second we were dismissed, I pivoted on my heel and marched over to Thomas and Luke.

"What did he say?" Luke asked.

"Katherine got herself appointed by CPS to represent Collier County," I said through gritted teeth.

"She's not that bad, James. I've had to deal with her on numerous occasions before we merged the packs."

"It's not that," I tried to say.

"Are you okay?" Thomas asked as my friend, not as my Alpha.

"I don't know," I told him honestly.

Of course there was a small part of me that was thrilled to spend time with her, but there was also the bigger part that equally resented and feared her rejection. My wolf was very attached to her and lately I'd been struggling to stay away. In some weird way this might be a blessing, or more like my own personal living hell.

Thomas gave a curt head nod, but I didn't need to turn around to feel her approach from behind me.

"I don't want to draw this out any more than you guys do," she said. "Thomas, it's good to see you. Luke, it's been a while."

"Yes, it has. It's been nice."

I could only imagine the look of death she was shooting his way. It should have brought me pleasure, but instead I was struggling not to growl at Luke.

This was never going to work.

Katherine simply chuckled. "I hear that a lot," she said dismissively. "James." She waited until I slowly turned to face her before continuing. "I'd like to get this over with as quickly as possible. Since the boys are already missing school for this, how about we head to Collier now and I can do a quick home inspection and talk to each of them. I'm sure we can all agree that the faster we get through this, the better."

"That'll be fine," Thomas assured her before I could respond.

I grit my teeth so hard I feared I might crack a molar as I glared at Thomas in warning.

"Great," she said, seemingly oblivious to my dark mood.

How could I feel her emotions so clearly and she not recognize mine in the least. It was infuriating and only affirmed the fact that a shifter and a human could never truly work.

I knew that after this nightmare was over, I was going to have to go into serious Katherine withdrawals and detox myself from her for a while. It was never easy, but for my sanity, when I got to the point of desperation and defense that I was currently working myself up to, it was time to stay away for a while, lest things get even harder.

I hated forcing myself into that, but she was like a drug to me, and I recognized the signs within myself enough to know I was building to my breaking point. That meant it was time for rehab.

Oh, I'd come running back to her again eventually, I always did, but I needed to get my head back in a better place first. That was if I could survive working alongside her until this case was over.

Her father had asked me to do it as a personal favor, but in truth, there was no way in hell my wolf or I would allow her to wander through a freaking wolf pack alone, and I sure wasn't about to entrust her safety to anyone else. I wasn't even certain I could submit that responsibility to Thomas himself.

"Well, come on, let's get this over with," I grumbled.

"Okay," she agreed.

Thomas shot me a worried look, but I chose to ignore it.

Much to my surprise, Katherine followed me outside and right to my car. As she stood next to the passenger door looking stubborn and determined, I barked at her.

"What are you doing?"

"Are you really going to let me just drive through your territory alone?"

I growled in frustration.

"No."

"I didn't think so. Do you want me to follow you or ride with you then?"

"Just get in the car," I snapped, feeling like I was barely hanging on by a thread.

Once we were both settled inside, I took a deep breath and felt an unusual calm settle over me as her scent enveloped me. I'd practically been holding my breath and steaming in irritation since the second she'd walked into that courtroom, but here, trapped in tight quarters, alone with her, I took it all in.

Closing my eyes, I just breathed and felt my body shiver as it settled with a rightness I didn't know how to describe. It was terrifying.

When I opened my eyes again, Katherine was watching me with open curiosity, but she didn't say a word.

She reached out and touched my arm.

"Hey, I know the last thing you want is to be stuck on a job with me. I'll make it as painless and quick as possible," she said softly.

There was a pain in her voice that nearly broke me.

I simply nodded as I put the car into drive and made my way home. As we crossed into Pack territory there was a rightness about having her there with me. It was wrong, and I couldn't allow myself to trust it, but it was there.

The radio in my car sounded.

"Um, boss. We've got a report out that Harlan is on the loose again."

I grabbed it and pressed the button.

"Shit. I don't have time for this."

"Should we call Thomas then? He's run off and we're having trouble tracking him."

Just then a large wolf stumbled out across the road and I had to swerve and slam on the breaks to avoid hitting him.

Dammit, Harlan.

"Oh no. Stop," Katherine screamed.

"What do you think I'm doing?"

She jumped from the car and took off running towards the drunken bastard.

"Deaton get your ass out here and get him. I'm dropping you his coordinates now. Asshole just tried to wreck me. Also note, I have a civilian with me so careful what you say over the radio, okay?"

I looked up in time to see Katherine's outstretched hand as she slowly approached Harlan.

"What the hell is she thinking?"

I tossed the radio onto the seat and jumped out to rescue her.

"Katherine! Are you insane? That's a wolf."

She shrugged. "He looks sick."

"Which is why you shouldn't approach him."

"He needs help, James."

Yeah, he certainly did, like a night in the dry tank to sleep off this latest bender. I couldn't tell her that though.

"Get out of here," I told Harlan who had the audacity to growl at me.

"Katherine, get back in the car. I'm calling animal control to take care of him. He'll be fine."

I glared at him refraining myself from growling back. Combined with the threat of animal control, it was enough. Harlan cowered and then tripped over his own two feet when he tried to turn and run.

"Get in the car, Katherine."

Much to my surprise, she listened.

"Harlan, you asshole, get out of the road. Deaton will be by to pick you up in a few minutes."

His head bobbed around like he could barely control it. I took that to mean he understood so I got back into the vehicle and drove away.

"We should have stayed with him until they arrived."

"It's fine. He'll be fine. I promise."

We were almost to Kayden's house when a call came through from Thomas.

"Yeah?" I answered.

"I've got Kayden, Kasen, and Eros with me. We're having a little chat before you bring Katherine by their houses. Give me an hour."

"Asshole," I muttered.

He just laughed.

"I really am sorry to do this to you, but it's important."

"Yeah fine."

I hung up on him and then turned to her.

"The boys are still back at the courthouse. Can you start the home inspection without them or should we wait?"

"I'd rather wait. How long do you think they'll be?"

"I don't know. Could be another hour or so."

She huffed in frustration.

"This isn't how these things are supposed to go."

"I'm aware."

A crackling sound came across my radio again.

"Sheriff, we've got Harlan secured."

"Good job."

"Should we keep him."

"Yeah, put him in a cell and let him sober up. I'll swing by his house and let Betty June know he's safe." I set down the radio and turned to Katherine. "Mind if I make a stop on the way?"

Katherine
Chapter 6

I shouldn't have jumped into the car with James. What had I been thinking?

While I was more than happy to actually spend some time with him, his scowls and short fuse with me confirmed that he still wanted nothing to do with me.

It nearly broke my heart and hurt my pride even further. It had been years since we'd last been alone together and I think a part of me was hoping the undeniable chemistry between us would somehow pull us back together if given the chance.

How wrong was I? He could barely stand to even look at me.

I wasn't prepared for the level of hostility I sensed in him. I couldn't tell if it was a war raging within him or towards me.

It wasn't like I hadn't seen him over the years. Every time I had I'd felt that connection to him, but now, it was like there was nothing but pain and regret.

I'd spent far too much time recently thinking about him. My pathetic attempt at dating again had resurfaced so much. Not to mention the nagging reminders my parents shamelessly dropped, that had my head swimming with this ridiculous notion that just maybe I was meant to be with James. Maybe we could rekindle what we'd had… what I single-handedly destroyed.

He pulled up to a small house painted a bright blue with a bold red door.

Parking in front of it, he got out then turned to bark at me. "Stay in the car. I'll just be a minute."

I rolled down the window feeling trapped, hurt, and alone.

He knocked on the front door and a small woman answered. She was wearing a housecoat and bunny slippers. Her graying hair was sticking out of a messy bun. They spoke for a moment and then she threw her arms around James who embraced her back.

The pain that sliced through my heart at the sight was tangible. It took everything in my power to sit there and watch. I certainly had never been a violent person before, but I was ready to knock this woman out.

I started to hyperventilate as blood pounded in my ears. The edges of my vision began to darken as he helped the woman into the backseat. I could feel her eyes boring holes into the back of my head.

I was seconds away from losing my shit.

James slid into the seat next to me and then cursed when he looked at me.

He grabbed my shoulders and shook me.

"Katherine, look at me," he demanded.

I looked into the depth of the endless blue pools I remembered so well. The sort of eyes I could lose myself in for days.

"Are you okay?"

Was I?

No. I was far from okay. I was plotting the homicide of a woman I didn't even know simply because she had hugged James when I couldn't.

Still, his touch seemed to soothe my soul and I started to relax.

"Are you okay?" he repeated again.

Slowly I nodded.

Clearing my throat, I even replied, "I'm okay."

Concern was etched into his handsome face. God, how had I ever let him go?

You didn't let him go, you kicked him to the curb. You practically threw him out the door along with all his things just because he had the audacity to love you.

I wanted to cry at the memory. He had been mine and I'd blown it. Now he could barely even look at me.

He didn't ask again, seeming satisfied by my response.

I was quiet as we drove along. No one else spoke either and when James pulled up to the local jail where I knew he must work, I wasn't sure if I should stay in the car or follow him. When he let the housecoat wearing hussy out, I knew I wasn't going to handle just letting the two of them walk away. I got out and followed quietly behind.

In the time we had dated, I'd never once seen where James worked. I had barely even set foot across the Collier County line. How could I not be curious now?

Inside the building was a small waiting area. I could see desks behind a partition of glass and a few rooms lining the far wall. To the right were several barred cells.

I gasped when I saw a large naked man standing in one of them.

"He's naked!" I blurted out.

The others in the room all looked my way and then collectively burst out laughing.

"Why'd you bring her, Sheriff," the man complained.

At first, I thought he was talking about me, but then the small woman we'd picked up stomped over to him and shoved a bag through the bars.

"Betty June, you know I have to search that first," one of the deputies said.

"You guys got this handled?" James asked.

"Yes, sir," another man sitting behind a desk said.

"Call me if they give you any trouble. Betty June, you promised me you'd behave. Give these boys any grief and you'll find yourself in the cell next to him."

There was a glint of trouble in the woman's eyes as she smiled back at him.

"Good luck," James told them as he placed his arm at the small of my back and led me back outside. "Sorry about that," he mumbled. "Unfortunately, they're regulars around here."

"Oh," I said before blurting out, "but why is he naked?"

James just laughed and shook his head.

"Come on, let's get out of here."

He looked down at his watch as we got back into the car and scowled.

"Have you ever been to Collier before?"

"Not outside of that one disaster of a date we had."

I watched him cringe just a little as I regretted my sharp word choice.

"Well, how about I give you a tour and then we'll try Kayden's again in hopes that he's back by then."

"Um, okay."

I sat, quietly taking in the beauty surrounding me. Collier was peppered with prime land and the views were to die for. It was shockingly different from anything I'd seen around here. Sure, we had the mountains in the distance and the valleys. The river ran through downtown, yet here the landscape wasn't peppered with buildings and factories, it was open, natural, raw.

"It's gorgeous," I said reverently as he pulled off the road and drove through a field to a set of large boulders by the river.

"This is probably my favorite place in the world. The guys and I basically grew up here."

"What guys?" I asked curiously.

His forehead furrowed like he thought I was crazy.

"The Six Pack."

I had never heard him refer to anyone like that before, of that I was positive.

"Who's that?"

"Only my best friends in the entire world. How do you not know this?"

I sighed and stared out the window for a moment.

"You never introduced me to any of your friends," I said softly. "Actually, you sort of forbade me to even ask about it. Anything regarding Collier was off-limits. I know nothing about your family or your life here."

He cringed.

I didn't want to hurt him, but it was simply the truth.

"I'm sorry," he surprised me by saying. "I never wanted to shut you out."

I nodded, hesitant to get my hopes up.

"So who are the Six Pack then?"

Much to my surprise, James relaxed and even smiled. I couldn't even believe what I was seeing. I'd missed that smile. I'd missed him.

"Well, obviously, there are six of us. We've been running together since we were in diapers. I'm closer to them than just about anyone." He hesitated and gave me a strange look before continuing. "My parents are alive and well. They're good people, but we're not all that close. I have two sisters as well. They are much older than me. I was sort of the accidental kid and I'm not certain my parents really wanted a third."

"I'm sure that's not true. How can they not be proud of everything you've accomplished?"

A funny look crossed his face, but he grinned and nodded.

"They are. It's just different than say your parents. But it's fine. I don't have anything against them. It's just that the Six Pack, my best friends, well, they're my true family."

I nodded. "Tell me about them?"

His Chosen Mate

Everything about James lit up. There was a lightness to him that I'd never experienced before. It made his already handsome features somehow sexier.

"Well, there's Wyatt. He's mat-uh-married to Kate. They've been together forever. He works out at the ranch while she owns Kate's Diner just outside of town. We passed it on the drive in."

I nodded, knowing the place.

"Then there's Clay who recently, uh, married Winnie. Clay's sort of the quiet one of the group, but he keeps us in line when we need it. He's great about making sure we don't go too long without catching up. Winnie's pretty good about that too, though she recently called in a 9-1-1 emergency when she found out it was his birthday and he hadn't told her." He laughed.

I struggled to see how that was funny.

"Isn't that an abuse of the system?"

"Absolutely, but to her it was a total emergency with a last-minute surprise party. Of course we all pulled it off for her."

Who was this guy? I'd never heard him talk about these people that very clearly meant a lot to him.

"Then there's Austin and Emmett. Both single. Austin's a clown and Emmett's an instigator. Together the two of them are often trouble."

"So that's four, plus you makes five. I'm assuming there's one more."

He nodded. "Thomas. He's probably my best friend in the entire world."

"Thomas Collier?" I asked as he nodded.

I knew Thomas was a major authority figure in the area. He was young for it, but then James was pretty young to be Sheriff too. I didn't understand the hierarchy of Collier, but I knew it was different than anything I was used to. There were very valid reasons why so many labeled them a big cult.

"Um, is Thomas married?"

59

"He is, to Lily. She's a hoot. You'd love her," he said affectionately.

For some reason that made me irrationally jealous. I didn't want to admit it even to myself, but I didn't like James talking about another woman with such obvious love.

I pushed those feelings aside and tried to commit to memory all the people he'd mentioned. This was more than he'd ever shared with me before.

When James and I were together he was very present and committed, but his personal life in Collier had been off-limits. He'd told me more than once that he would give it all up and walk away to be with me.

I'd have to admit, that had freaked me out a bit and made me question the validity of the cult theory. I didn't know why he was opening up now, but I was glad for it.

What James and I had had together was almost primal. The sex was indescribable, and I knew that nothing else would ever compare. The pull I felt towards him was undeniable, even now, all these years later as we sat quietly looking out over the water and beyond to the fields.

Just being with him brought a peace and comfort I only ever felt in his presence. It would be so easy to fall prey to that once more.

Would that really be so bad?

"Okay, enough about that. We'll do a drive through town and start making those house calls so I can get you out of here. People around here don't really take kindly to outsiders, especially court appointed ones," he admitted.

"I'll keep a low profile. No one needs to know why I'm here, James."

He barked out a laugh as he fired up his car and pulled away.

"Trust me, they know. Word travels quickly in a… uh… small town."

I didn't question it or bother to ask, knowing I wasn't going to get answers anyway. He had always talked sort of cryptic about this place and that certainly hadn't changed despite a brief pause in his shield to share about his friends with me.

Instead, I stayed quiet, looking out the window as we drove along.

"Is that a barn?" I asked curiously.

"Yeah, one of several. They house horses here. The next one we pass will be a lot bigger and that's the dairy. Clay and one of Thomas's sisters run it. We've had a lot of expansion over the last several years."

"They're so well kept and picturesque. It's beautiful."

He smiled and nodded. "Yes, it is. I used to think I could just turn my back on this place and walk away, but now, I'm not so sure I ever could have."

My heart ached knowing exactly what he meant.

He'd once agreed to do just that, for me.

Maybe in some way, this was the closure both of us needed. But the thought of walking away from this man forever didn't sit well with me. Actually, it made me angry as my anxiety started to spike.

James pulled over on the side of the road.

"Hey, are you okay?"

"What? Of course," I lied. "Why would you even ask?"

He watched me closely and I knew that he knew I was lying, but he didn't say anything as he resolutely put the car back in gear and kept driving.

Was I okay?

No! There was nothing okay about any of this. The attraction I'd always felt towards him was still there, perhaps even stronger.

My body was overly heated, and I felt like I might just combust internally when he looked my way.

I wanted him.

I couldn't deny that. Despite everything, I still wanted this man with a desperation that I didn't know how to contain. But we weren't kids anymore and I couldn't afford to just fall into his arms or his bed no matter how much I wanted to.

It would be so easy to give in to that desire too. Something told me that James wouldn't put up a protest either. My only hesitation was the fear that this time I wouldn't survive losing him again.

As we came into a cute little town that looked like something out of a Hallmark movie, my internal conflict subsided to open curiosity.

It was hard not to notice the names: Thomas Street, Collier Street, Zachary Street. I knew that Zachary Collier was Thomas's father who had run things around here until one day he seemed to disappear, and Thomas stepped up. I honestly wasn't sure if the man was even still alive.

Many of the stores and places around town were Collier this or Collier that. The streets were pristine to the point of bordering creepy. I'd never really seen anything like it, except maybe in movies. Did places like this actually exist though?

We passed by the tavern that Allen had tried to take me to. I pursed my lips in frustration that he would even jump into my head to disrupt an otherwise good day. I didn't want to think of him. I wanted to just stay in this moment with James, maybe forever, and that both thrilled and terrified me.

James

Chapter 7

Katherine's mood swings were giving me whiplash.

I shouldn't be able to feel them with such certainty. Watching her look out across town, I couldn't even fathom what was frustrating her so much. She was borderline freaking out on me, but I had no clue why.

On the exterior she was the epitome of cool, calm, and collected, but on the inside, she was a mass of nerves and emotions.

It wasn't like I could just ask her about it, especially when she was going to great lengths not to react outwardly. I'd already slipped up once and she was smart enough to catch on if I kept it up.

I was going to see if she wanted to stop by the tavern for a drink but sensing her discomfort, I kept driving. As I passed the Alpha house and noticed Thomas's truck out front, I assumed it was safe to proceed.

Ending our tour, I drove over to Kayden's house.

"Which one is this?" she asked.

"Kayden."

She pulled out a file from her bag and read through it. "Okay. Are you escorting me inside and hanging out as well?" she asked dryly.

"I can wait out here if you prefer, but it will probably go smoother if I come inside."

"They don't like outsiders. Yeah, yeah, I got it."

I gave her an apologetic look. No one wished she wasn't considered an outsider more than me. And I hadn't wanted to be put in this situation playing escort and entertaining her today, but I damn well wasn't going to entrust anyone else to do it either.

Biting down the desire to run around and open the door for her, I leaned against the hood of the car and waited for her to get out.

"Ready?"

"Of course," she said coolly, having switched from my Katherine, to emotional Katherine, to business Katherine in a matter of minutes.

I sighed, then led the way to the front door and knocked.

Janet answered.

"James?"

"Hey Janet. Did Thomas explain that we'd be coming around? This is Katherine Carter. She's with Child Protective Services. Don't be alarmed by that, it's just a formality for Kayden's court case," I assured her.

She nodded even while cutting hesitant eyes towards Katherine.

"Thomas told us."

"Is Kayden here?" Katherine asked calmly with a friendly smile on her face.

"Please don't take my boy away. He didn't mean no harm," she practically begged.

Katherine softened next to me.

"I have no reason to believe there will be a need for that. This really is just a formality. May I have a look around the house? And then I'd like to talk to Kayden and hear his side of the story. You're welcome to stay by my side through it all."

Janet looked up to me for permission and I nodded my reassurance.

"Okay then. Come on in."

Inside, the house was clean and tidy with a livable feel to it. Kayden sat quietly at the kitchen table looking terrified, as he should be, while Janet showed Katherine around.

"This is Kayden's room," she finally said proudly as I held back to try and calm Kayden down.

"Am I in big trouble?" he asked me.

"Nah. We'll get this all sorted."

"But CPS is here. She could take me away, throw me in juvie. We didn't mean any harm, Sheriff."

"Kayden, she's not taking you away. I've got this handled, okay?"

"Oh do you?" Katherine asked, making me jump.

I turned sheepishly to find her standing there with her arms crossed over her chest as Janet paled beside her.

"Uh…"

"You can wait outside, Sheriff," she said with full authority, but then she winked down at Kayden. "Unless Kayden would like for you to stay."

The kid sighed in relief and nodded.

"He can stay."

"This shouldn't take long. I just need for you to be honest with me here, okay?"

"I can do that."

"Your mom's pretty great, isn't she?" she surprised me by asking as she took a seat across from the boy.

This clearly threw him off as well, but he beamed up at his mother and nodded.

"She's the best."

"Is the house always this clean?"

He nodded emphatically.

"Always. Mom insists on it."

"And where's your dad?"

Kayden blanched and gulped hard.

"He's at work. He's a ranch hand."

"Are you scared of your father, Kayden?" she asked with concern.

I knew the man and he was harmless, a hard worker, and a loving husband and father. Never once had any of them caused trouble before.

"I mean, I guess, a little. I'm not like scared he'll hurt me or anything, more scared I'm disappointing him. He was really upset with this mess I made."

"Why don't you tell me exactly what happened."

He shrugged and his head drooped.

"Kasen's mom dropped us off at the movies and we got some popcorn and drinks and went inside to watch it. There weren't a lot of people in there, and it was a really dumb movie. We got bored and started talking. Someone down front fussed at us and Eros threw some popcorn at him. It didn't hit him or anything, but the guy got mad and went to get Mr. Terrence. He made us leave but when we asked for a refund he refused."

"How did that make you feel?"

He shrugged again.

"We weren't happy about it but understood why he was doing it. Still, Kasen's mom wasn't picking us up until after the movie was over, so we didn't have anywhere to go or anything to do."

"Why didn't you just call her?"

He shrugged yet again. I couldn't help but wonder if I acted like this when I was fourteen. Probably. Even then my friends and I thought we ruled the world.

"We just hung around outside instead. Eros saw a spigot on. It was dripping water and he pulled out a bag of balloons, and we filled them up and threw them against the wall."

"I see."

"It was just water balloons. We weren't trying to actually damage anything. We were just wasting time while we waited, but then that cop drove up and caught us. He said we were going to be in big trouble. I believed him."

I felt like there was something more to the story, but when Katherine prompted him, that's all he would say about it. Apparently, Dixon read them the riot act, ticketed them, and then left. It was all in line with the camera footage I'd seen, but I couldn't help but feel like there was something missing.

Katherine jotted down some notes and then said goodbye.

"Thank you, Kayden, and don't worry. I won't be recommending you go anywhere."

"You mean it?"

She nodded. "I can see your remorse over how you handled things. I have a feeling next time you'll choose a different path."

"There won't be a next time, will there, Kayden?" Janet asked him sternly.

"No ma'am. Not for me."

Both women smiled and shared a knowing nod.

Yeah, he was a good kid and didn't deserve any of the crap Bucky and Dixon were trying to put him through.

We said goodbye and left the house.

Once back in the car she turned to me and smirked.

"That really wasn't that bad, was it?"

"Nope."

"I can't believe you were ready to fight me over this."

"I didn't fight you."

"But you wanted to," she said with certainty.

"But I didn't. I know when to retreat. Your father wasn't going to side with me on this one."

She snarled at the reminder.

"Because I was right," she muttered.

I chose to ignore it and remained quiet on the drive over to Kasen's house.

We approached the scene exactly the same as we had with Kayden, only while Katherine took the tour of the house, I couldn't help but notice how the kid squirmed in his seat, especially when she went into his bedroom.

"You okay?" I finally asked him.

"Yeah. Of course. Nothing to hide here. Just nervous. I've never been in trouble like this before."

That was certainly a plausible explanation, but my gut told me there was something more. As Katherine sat down across from him for their little chitchat, I couldn't help but notice how precise his retelling of the story was to Kayden's. Of course I expected the two boys to share similar stories, but everyone's perspective is a little different. There's no way around that, it's what makes us individuals, yet their retellings were nearly word for word the same, especially when it came to Dixon.

"Thanks Kasen. I'll be in touch if I need anything more."

"That's it?" he blurted out.

"That's it," she confirmed.

The relief in the boy's body was evident.

Katherine rose, thanked his mother for her side of the story and walked out. I turned and ran after her to keep up.

"That's it?" I asked back in the car. "But it was clear he wasn't telling you something."

"I know."

"You know? And you didn't press him for it?"

"James, these boys are terrified. They've never been in any kind of trouble before, not even a bad report from school. Nothing. They're scared and despite what people think about my job, I'm not in the habit of frightening kids. I advocate for them. I'm on their side, always. That's my job. I am not some boogieman who sneaks in at night and snatches children from their homes, though I know there's a reputation of just that. I'm not going to get anywhere without a little trust and cooperation. Clearly, that isn't coming today, but it will."

I was really impressed by her words. I'd never really thought of it like that before. In truth, even I had hated her job, looking at her more like an enemy than an ally when it came to protecting the kids in my Pack.

Had I been so very wrong about that?

She sighed. "I've worked with Eros before. He used to live over in Larken Trailer Park before it burned down. I'm surprised to even see him living here, yet I suppose I shouldn't be since Luke Larken and Thomas Collier seem suddenly tight. Want to explain that to me?"

"Nope."

There was no way I could explain to my very human mate how two feuding Alphas made a peace alliance to join the Packs together as one.

"Figured," she mumbled.

I pretended not to hear her.

"So Eros has given you grief before."

"Yeah. He fell in with a bad crowd at school for a while and it was brought to my attention, though it's been some time now. I imagine it likely stopped about the time he moved here?"

I shrugged. "I'm not sure. He's never given me any problems."

It was true. Most of the Larken kids had straightened up quickly, grateful for a change and upgrade in life by moving into Collier.

Katherine shook her head as we turned on to Larken Lane.

"Let me guess, most from Larken Trailer Park now live on this road?"

I scowled. "So?"

"Collier isn't exactly known for its hospitality, so I have to wonder, just why would you guys take in such a riff-raff group of troublemakers?"

"They aren't troublemakers," I protested. "They were just down on their luck."

She seemed to consider that, though I was happy when she dropped the conversation as we reached our final destination.

Katherine

Chapter 8

These boys weren't the only ones keeping secrets around here. I knew there was much more going on than James was admitting to. No way would Collier just openly accept a bunch of misfit strays like this. Not without a damn good reason.

I hadn't exaggerated anything when I'd explained to Allen just how unwelcoming the whole lot of them was. Still, I knew better than to press James for anything more.

As he pulled up in front of a brand-new two-story house, my jaw dropped open.

I grabbed Eros's folder and triple checked the address.

"What's wrong?" he finally asked.

"I saw firsthand the conditions this boy was living in. I know his parents, James, and what they do for a living. There is no way they can suddenly afford all of this. Something isn't right here."

He sighed. "Don't read too much into that. Thomas was very generous when helping them relocate. We'd already built this neighborhood, but no one was living in it yet so it was used as temporary housing after the trailer park burned down. They were given jobs at the ranch and the dairy saw expansions with the need for extra hands. With the new income for the… uh… town and individuals, they were given the option to buy. That's what you're seeing here. Nothing more."

"But why?" I demanded.

It didn't make any sense at all. Why would Collier reach out and help like that? Why would Thomas even want to invest in the sort of troublemakers I knew came from that run down park?

"We take care of our own, Katherine."

That's all he had to say to me? As if I wasn't fully aware of that to begin with.

"But they weren't your kind," I blurted out.

There had been no signs of commonality between Larken Park and Collier County. If anything, it felt as if they were fighting against each other, and now this?

James's jaw locked and I knew I wasn't going to get any of the answers I sought. Not now, not ever. He was an unbreachable fortress when he got like this and I knew that whatever the hell was going on around here, I wasn't about to be brought into the loop.

Trying to let go of my frustrations, I got out of the car and headed for the front door. I didn't even wait for James.

I knocked and waited. By the time Shell opened the door, James had caught up to me.

Her cheeks blushed and she gave me an apologetic look. I could sense her fear of my presence and I hated it. The last time I'd seen Shell and Eros she had sworn to me it would be the last. This wasn't the same, but I couldn't blame her from freaking out about it.

"Katherine, I swear, he's changed. He's not in that life anymore and hasn't caused any trouble since we got here."

"Is Deek home?"

"No ma'am. He's at work. Should I call him? Do we need a lawyer?"

"Shell, relax," I said, trying to assure her with a hug. "This is just routine."

"You mean Eros isn't in trouble?"

I shrugged. "That depends on how honest he's willing to be with me. Can I take a quick tour of the new house?"

She beamed proudly. "Absolutely."

We chatted as she showed me around. I had to admit it was really nice. I couldn't imagine how they could possibly afford it, but I wasn't here to judge that. I was only here for her son's protection.

"Hi Ms. Carter," Eros said as he sat at the kitchen table looking sad.

"Hi Eros. It's nice to see you again."

"No, it's not nice. You told me if you ever had to come to my house again that you'd take me away."

I tried not to smile. It had been nothing more than a threat to whip this poor lost little boy back on the right track and until now it had seemed to work.

"Maybe we can forget about that."

"Really?"

"Well, yeah. You've been doing really well, or so I assume. I haven't heard a peep from you in over two years. What changed, sweetie? Why now?"

"Nothing. I swear. We weren't really doing nothing wrong."

"Why don't we start from the beginning, okay?"

He nodded swiping tears from his eyes. It broke my heart.

"Eros, I need you to take a deep breath and relax. I know enough of what happened to know you aren't going anywhere, okay? This is just a formality so I can help get this charge wiped off of your file completely. Do you hear me? I'm on your side, kiddo. I'm always on your side."

He nodded, relaxing just a little.

"Okay."

"Can you tell me exactly what happened?"

"Yup," and then he proceeded to tell me exactly what happened, exactly as the other two boys had told their story.

When he was done, I patted him on the arm.

"We're friends, right?"

"I guess."

"There's more to this story, isn't there? Because that was pretty much exactly what Kayden and Kasen told me too."

"But that's good right? All of our stories match? We're telling the truth."

"I do believe you are all telling the truth, but I also feel like there's more to it than what you're giving me."

His eyes widened and he gulped hard.

I knew I was right.

"You're not going to be in trouble for telling the truth," James explained. "It's okay. Ms. Carter and I need all the information if we're going to protect you."

"I don't want anyone to get in trouble," he whispered.

"I can't promise you that won't happen, but we also can't help if we don't know what really happened. Do you understand?"

He was so kind and patient with the boy that it softened my gooey heart towards him even more.

"Can you tell me how Kasen got a black eye?" I asked.

The shock on the kid's face was evident.

"He told you about that?"

I didn't confirm or deny his question. Kasen hadn't said a word to me, but while his mother was giving me a tour of her house, she'd mentioned it. When she'd dropped him off, her son had been fine, but when she picked the boys up, he was sporting a noticeably swollen black eye.

"We aren't supposed to talk about that," Eros whispered.

"Who told you that?" James demanded.

The boy shook his head begging with his eyes not to make him say anything more.

"Do I need to get Thomas and Luke down here?"

Eros started breathing heavy trying not to freak out.

"No, sir."

"Then answer the question. Who gave Kasen a black eye? Was it you?"

"No, sir."

"Calm down, sweetie," I told him. "We just need to know what happened, what *really* happened."

He looked to his mother for help.

"Whatever it is, you have to tell them."

The fight fled him. I could see it in his sagging shoulders.

"We were cutting up in the movie and someone got mad. They got Mr. Terrence who kicked us out. We were just hanging around on the side of the building waiting for Kasen's mom to pick us up."

"We've heard all of this before," James interrupted.

I put a hand on his arm to stop him.

"Let him talk, please."

We were finally getting somewhere, or at least I hoped we were.

"We weren't mad or anything, just bored. I saw a spigot dripping along the wall and I had a pocket full of water balloons already. I filled a few up and threw them against the wall. Kayden and Kasen joined in. We weren't trying to destroy anything. It was just water. We kept throwing them, trying to see who could get it up the highest. That was all."

"That's not what Officer Dixon said," James mentioned and neither of us mentioned the way the boy shrunk at the mention of his name.

"You've all said the same thing, that Officer Dixon saw you throwing stuff at the building and drove up to fuss at you. He gave you tickets and sent you on your way. Is that what happened?" I asked.

He started to nod, but then slowed and shook it.

"The dash cam didn't have the sound turned on, but it looked like he got out and yelled at you. What did he really say?"

Eros had tears in eyes. "I can't say," he whispered.

"Eros, honey, please. You have to tell them. Katherine's helped us before, remember? She kept you from being taken from me. You can trust her. I'm not going to let anything bad happen to you."

"Your mom's right, Eros. Nothing bad comes with telling the truth."

"That's not what he said."

"What did he say?" I asked.

"I don't want my friends getting in trouble either."

"Eros, please," his mother begged.

He finally broke down and told us quite a different story.

"It's true he came over and fussed at us. I already told the guys we had to clean up the balloon mess and we tried to explain that to him. I told him we didn't mean anything by it and didn't want any trouble, but he yelled at us anyway and he did give us a ticket. That's all on camera just like he said."

"But something else happened after that, didn't it?"

He nodded.

"He went back to his car and I guess he was doing some paperwork or something and then he was smoking."

"Okay."

"It wasn't a cigarette. Kasen noticed it first and pointed it out. Kayden asked him if he was smoking a joint while Kasen insisted it wasn't legal and we were going to tell if he didn't take away the stupid ticket."

"Um, that's kind of blackmailing an officer," James casually mentioned.

I shushed him. I needed to hear what else happened.

"What happened next?" I encouraged him to proceed.

Eros sighed like the weight of the world was on his little shoulders.

"He turned the camera off and got back out of the car. 'What did you say?' he asked us. 'Nothing,' I tried to say, but Kasen told him he was going to be in big trouble for smoking a joint on the job."

"How did Officer Dixon react to that?"

"He hauled off and slapped Kasen across the face. Gave him a black eye and everything."

"Then what happened?" James asked.

I could feel his aggression levels rise. He was pissed listening to this story. I was too, but feeling his heightened emotional state combined with my own was making it very hard for me to stay impartial and not react to what Eros was telling us.

"And after that?" I echoed James's sentiment.

"He made us promise not to say a word or he'd see to it that we went straight to jail. Then he got back in his car, flicked the joint out the window right at us, and drove away."

"There's none of this on camera. I've seen it myself," James whispered to me.

"I told you he turned it off. He told us that. He made sure we knew it was just our word against his and no one would believe a couple of punk kids like us."

"I believe you," I assured him.

"I can attempt a case but without hard evidence it's going to be a tough sell," he admitted.

"Hard evidence? Like the joint?" Eros asked.

We both turned to stare at him.

"You have the joint?" his mother demanded causing him to shrink in his seat a little more.

"I don't, Mom! I swear! But Kasen was so angry. His mom was going to be there soon though, so we all picked up the balloon mess and cleaned up before walking around front to wait for her. The joint wasn't there when we were done."

"What happened to it?" James blurted out.

"I don't know for sure, but I think Kayden or Kasen might have taken it as evidence."

"Come on. We have to go speak with the other boys again. If we can find that joint and match DNA to Dixon on it then suddenly I've got a viable case again."

"You did the right thing in telling us, Eros," I assured him, giving his mother a hug on our way out.

"I did? I'm not in bigger trouble for it?"

"No way, kiddo. We've got this from here. If I need anything further or James needs an official statement, we'll be in touch. Otherwise, I think we're done here."

James was already in the car waiting. He even turned his siren on and raced back to Kayden's house.

I jumped out of the car as soon as it stopped, feeling the adrenaline of our high-speed drive to get there.

James ran ahead of me and banged on the door.

Poor Janet looked terrified when she opened the door, and I couldn't blame her.

"We need to speak with Kayden again."

"James, you're freaking me out. What happened?"

"Is he here?"

I could see Kayden peeking out from the hallway.

"Hey Kayden. We have a few more questions to ask you regarding a joint you might have picked up," I said calmly.

Poor kid looked like a wild animal ready to bolt, but at the mention of the joint, he froze like a deer caught in headlights.

"I don't have it. I swear."

"Does Kasen have it?" James asked.

"I don't know for sure, but I think so."

"Come on," he said, grabbing my hand and pulling me away from the house.

"What is going on here?" Janet yelled after us.

All I could concentrate on was the feel of his hand linked with mine.

He helped me to the car, and I instantly missed the connection when he let go to run around to the driver's side as we sped off for Kasen's house.

James pounded on the door, but from the look of the woman's face as she answered the door, Kasen was already gone.

"Where is he?"

"Please, he's not in trouble. We really are trying to help."

"He was just here, but Kayden called him, and he took off out back."

"Stay here. I'll find him," James said as he ran out of the back door.

"Did he take anything with him?" I asked.

She shook her head. "Not that I know of."

"Great, would it be okay with you if I checked his room again?"

"What are you looking for?"

"Marijuana."

"No way. Kasen's a good boy. He's not into drugs," she assured me.

"It's not his. It's possible evidence."

"I would know if it were here," she insisted. "There's nothing."

Still, together we checked coming up empty-handed.

"Where could he have put it?"

"I don't know what the other boys said, but Kasen isn't into drugs."

"No one's accusing him of that, but if we find this joint it could help their case and give us the answers we need, like how your son got that black eye."

She was suddenly much more cooperative as she led me outside to a fort in the backyard. I saw her sniff the air as if she somehow expected to smell it. No one had that great a sense of smell.

She climbed up the ladder waving me off when I tried to join her until at last, she pulled out a Ziploc baggie with a half smoked joint inside.

"I can't believe it. Not Kasen."

"There's a lot more to this story," I assured her as she passed it to me.

About ten minutes later James returned with Kasen, Kayden, and Eros.

"We found it," I announced.

The boys looked like they were going to throw up.

"Thank God, because these three are locking up on me again."

He passed the boys to Kasen's mom for her to deal with and then took the bag from me.

"Come on. I need to get this over to the lab. It takes a few days to get the results back and I'd like this case cleared up before we reconvene next week."

James

Chapter 9

I couldn't believe she found it.

When I'd caught up to the boys, they had been scared out of their minds. I tried to assure them they were not in any trouble, but I couldn't fault them for not trusting me. I was a cop too and they had clearly experienced something traumatic at Dixon's hand. He wouldn't get away with it. I was going to see to that personally.

It wasn't until I pulled up to the jail that I even realized I was driving one handed and holding Katherine's with the other. It was the most natural thing in the world. Being with her again just felt right.

"We made a good team today," I told her. "Just give me a minute to drop this off and get things rolling and I'll take you home."

She nodded but didn't seem to be able to formulate words as she stared down at our conjoined hands.

I wanted to ask her what she was thinking, but I didn't dare.

Instead, I left her sitting there as I went inside, pulled out an evidence bag and shoved the entire baggie inside it before passing it off to Deaton.

"I cannot stress the importance of this enough. I need a full DNA test run on this thing."

"Do we know who you think it goes to?"

"Last name Dixon. He's a new local cop, but comes from Chicago, I think."

"Got it. I'll let you know what we get back."

"Thanks."

"Are you on call tonight?"

"No. Julian takes over tonight. And I have to head back into town to take Katherine home, so only reach out if there's an emergency."

"You got it, sir."

It wasn't until I was back in the car and driving away from town that it dawned on me that I was still in my uniform. I kept spare clothes at the office and hadn't even thought to change.

"Are you in a hurry to get home?"

"Not particularly. Why?"

"I'm officially off duty after several days on call and I'd really like to get out of this uniform."

I didn't miss the way her eyes darted down my body as if she was just noticing what I was wearing for the first time. And I knew she liked what she saw. I could smell the spike of her arousal as it hit me hard.

Damn, this was probably a bad idea.

I'd just spent the entire day with her and the rightness of that hadn't gone unnoticed.

Mine, my wolf growled in my head as I clenched my jaw.

"Are you saying what I think you're saying?"

"What do you think I'm saying?" I dared to ask.

"You're stopping by your house?"

"Oh, uh, yeah. Is that okay with you?"

"You're actually going to let me see your house?"

"Don't make such a big deal of it. I'll just be a minute."

"Can I come in?"

"What? You've seen where I live before?"

"Uh, no, I haven't."

"Katherine we were practically living together," I reminded her, trying to recall if she was right or not. Surely, I'd brought her home at some point.

"James, you moved in with me. Those boundaries were set firm and your house, hell, basically the entirety of Collier County was off limits."

I frowned. Was she right? Maybe.

"Just forget it."

"No way. I swear today feels like a dream, like it can't possibly be real."

"Exaggerate much?" I teased rolling my eyes.

Still, I drove home. I'd meant to tell her to stay in the car, but the second I pulled to a stop, she was out of the vehicle and heading for my front door.

I groaned.

This was a very, *very* bad idea.

Being with her today only heightened my desire for her. I couldn't afford for that to happen. I already knew that detoxing myself from her was going to be so much harder this time.

Unlocking the door, I stepped aside and let her go ahead of me. For a wolf, it was the ultimate sign of respect and something I would only ever do for my Alpha, or my mate.

Mate, my wolf howled again.

I still didn't know how it was possible, but somewhere along the way I'd accepted it as truth. That didn't change anything though.

The second she was inside she started snooping around not even bothering to hide her curiosity. I just smiled as I walked back to the bedroom to change.

As I stripped down to my boxers, the phone rang, and I looked down to see it was Thomas. I knew I had to fill him in on what we'd found.

"Hey."

"How'd it go today?"

"Good actually," I said as I caught him up on everything we'd learned.

"It's going to take a lot for me not to drive over there and rip this guy's throat out for laying a hand on one of my kids."

"I know, but you have to trust me on this and let the system work. I'm on it."

"Okay," he reluctantly conceded. "Now how did things go today?"

"I already told you."

"I meant with your mate."

I nearly choked as I looked around waiting for her to magically appear or something.

"Oh, that."

"Yeah, *that*. So?"

"It's fine. I've got everything handled."

The door to my bedroom swung open and Katherine stood there frozen as she looked me up and down. I wasn't sure I'd ever felt so exposed, but my body instantly responded to the heated look in her eyes.

"I'll call you back later," I told Thomas, hanging up before he could even respond.

Every ounce of willpower in me snapped.

I practically stalked her like prey as I got up and walked towards the doorway where she stood. Her eyes dropped to the bulge of my boxers making my dick jump.

Uncertainty clouded my judgement until she licked her goddamn lips.

In seconds I had her in my arms and my lips crushed against hers like a starving man.

I knew those perfect lips. It had been too long, and kissing Katherine felt like coming home. I couldn't have stopped myself if I tried.

Resolved to my fate, I lifted her in my arms as her legs wrapped around my waist. I meant to take her to my bed, but somehow ended up with her back pressed against the wall instead as she moaned and ground herself against me.

It was sheer bliss feeling her around me and I was not strong enough to fight it, even knowing how much harder it would be to walk away from her. It would appear I was a man set on digging my own grave, but what a way to go.

With her back braced against the wall, I pulled back and looked down at her. Her hair was mussed, and her lips swollen. Her chest rose and fell with heavy breaths. She was still wearing the suit she'd had on in court this morning, though she had shed her jacket somewhere along the way.

Her skirt was already up around her waist, and it would be so easy to reach down between us, push her panties to the side, and take her fast and furiously. A primal need within me wanted just that, but I didn't know if I'd ever have this opportunity again. I still remembered all the reasons we shouldn't be together, but here and now, none of that mattered.

"Mine," I growled as I ripped her shirt off her body sending buttons flying in all directions.

Her eyes lit with awareness as she leaned forward to fist her hands in my hair and kiss me like she was seconds away from claiming me. That wasn't possible though, was it?

As her tongue darted past my lips to tangle with mine, all conscious thought fled me.

I reached around and undid the clasp of her bra letting it slip down her arms between us.

When she leaned back once more to dispose of it herself, I got a thorough look at her perfect tits. They were a little fuller than I remembered and the dark pink around her nipples called to me.

I growled again as I lowered my head and sucked one stiff point into my mouth to swirl my tongue around it as I sucked and savored first one and then the other until she was shaking in my arms and moaning in pleasure.

I reached down and pushed at my boxers until my cock sprang free.

Unable to deny her pleasure or my own for even a second longer, I pushed her panties aside and pressed myself into her in one swift thrust.

She gasped as I stilled, allowing her body time to adjust, but when her lips touched mine once more, there was no holding back as I took her hard and fast against the wall.

The sound of her crying out my name as her nails scraped across my back nearly pushed me over the cliff as she came hard in my arms.

Somehow, I managed to stave off my own orgasm. It was a blissful combination of pleasure and pain.

I carried her to my bed and gently laid her down before pulling out of her and standing back to admire her beauty.

Her muscles shook and she was completely disheveled. I'd never seen anything so beautiful.

Taking my time now, I slowly removed the remainder of her clothes and kicked off my boxers that were still pooled around my ankles until we were both gloriously naked.

"Mate," I whispered as I looked at her with longing.

Before she could question it, I began a slow and leisurely path trailing kisses over every inch of her body until she came again, first on my tongue, and then on my hand.

"Oh God. James," she cried.

The right thing to do would probably be to allow her to rest, but I couldn't. My need for her was too strong.

"I can't," she tried to say.

"Oh yes, you can," I assured her as I settled over her body and took her once more.

She was swollen and overly sensitive now, so I wasn't surprised when she started quickly building to yet another orgasm. But I didn't rush things like before.

Slow and steady we moved as one as I kissed her softly and murmured her name reverently.

We'd always been great at sex, but this was something different, nearly other-worldly. I knew I would remember this moment for the rest of my life.

Tears pricked her eyes at the beauty of it as I poured all my love into her. When a tear fell from her eyes, I kissed away the salty trail.

When her hips started bucking against me in search of her next release, I knew this perfect moment would be ending far too soon.

"Eyes on me," I whispered when they started to drift closed.

I couldn't say the words on the tip of my tongue. I had to hide my smile as my canines started to elongate demanding I claim her as mine, but with my actions and in my heart, I branded her soul to mine with the scorching heat of the moment.

When I couldn't hold out any longer, I picked up my pace and sought my own release as I brought her to another climax, only closing my eyes and breaking our connection as I collapsed down on her chest.

She was gasping for breath and crying softly as I rolled to my side and gathered her up into my arms so I could just hold her.

We were two hearts meant to beat as one, but from two different worlds destined to keep us apart.

Katherine
Chapter 10

I hadn't meant to fall asleep, and I certainly hadn't meant to cry in front of him. He'd sent my emotions into a spiraling rollercoaster that I hadn't been prepared for.

The room around me was dark. It smelled of sex, beautiful sex.

I nibbled on my swollen lip as I let myself remember it.

He was amazing. How had I ever let this man go? How was I going to walk away from him now?

As beautiful as our reunion had been, and how oddly perfect the unexpected day with James had gone, we still had a history that couldn't be overlooked.

We'd both done and said things in the past to hurt the other. We had been young and dumb, unprepared for love, but that wasn't something that could just disappear with a romp in the sheets, a completely amazing, mind-blowing romp in the sheets, but nonetheless could not fix our past.

"Mine," he whispered even in his sleep as he reached for me.

I should have gotten up and found my way home. I should have covered myself and protected my heart from any further damage this night could do, but instead, I rolled back to him resting my head on his bare chest and wrapping my body around him.

"Mine," I whispered back to him under the cover of darkness feeling the rightness of that word as I allowed myself to drift off back to sleep.

*****

I groaned and stretched.

Somewhere off in the distance I heard a knocking sound followed by voices. My eyes shot up as my heart raced. Looking around the room I didn't recognize anything. It took me a moment to get my bearing straight.

James!

He was still snoring softly beside me.

"James, come on. Don't be a bitch. Lily brought breakfast and everything," a male voice yelled from down the hall. "I'll check the bedroom," he said as I shook James trying to wake him.

"James. James, someone's in the house," I whispered.

He started to stir and then wrapped one powerful arm around me and crushed me back down against him.

"Come on James. I know spending the day with Katherine yesterday had to have screwed with your head. I'm not going to just let you pine and wallow for her all day, so get up."

Those last three words came out much slower than the rest as Thomas Collier stood there in the doorway staring down at us in surprise.

I squeaked and tried to grab for a blanket to cover myself only to find that we were still lying on top of the thing, so I grabbed a pillow instead.

James sat up quickly covering me with his own body and growled at the intruder.

"I mean, if she really is his true mate, then he has every right to pine and wallow all he wants. And then man the hell up and do something about it. Regardless, this preggers mama needs to eat so get your asses out here now. I mean it, I'm not waiting."

No one moved as I looked between James and Thomas uncertain what silent encounter was transpiring between them.

A woman with a protruding round belly and short blonde hair highlighted in pink pushed past Thomas. Her jaw dropped open in surprise.

"Oh shit. Please tell me you're Katherine or else things just got *super* weird."

"I am," I managed to say, thinking things were already super weird.

The woman shrugged. "Well, okay then. No harm done. Get dressed and come on. I'm starving."

She turned and walked away grabbing Thomas's hand and dragging him with her back to the kitchen.

I sat there in shock trying to process everything I'd just heard. They were clearly worried about James having spent the day with me. Why? So many questions were running through my head. What did she mean by a true mate? I'd never heard the term before, yet recognition fluttered in my chest.

James had called me 'mate' when we were having sex last night. What the hell did that even mean?

He sighed watching me process through everything.

"They just worry about me. Try not to read too much into it," he said softly as he got out of bed and strode over to his dresser, pulling out two pairs of fresh boxers, a pair of sweatpants, and a large T-shirt. He tossed one of the underwear and the shirt to me while he put on the rest.

I just sat there staring at him with a million things going through my mind.

"Please don't overthink this. Are you hungry?"

I slowly nodded.

He sniffed the air. "No doubt she made more than enough for all of us."

I sniffed the air. There was a faint hint of bacon, but that was it.

"Um, okay. I'll be out in just a minute."

I grabbed the clothes and ran for the bathroom, locking the door behind me. For a minute I just paced back and forth. What the hell was going on?

Oh my gosh! I slept with James, my James!

That reality was hitting me hard.

"Guys, just go. She's freaking out enough already," I heard James say to his friends. "Stop worrying about me. I'm fine."

So much had happened in such a short time, and I'd just gotten caught up in the moment. We both had.

If I let myself think back through the night, I was definitely going to freak out, like how I had sex with James, not just sex that happened to be extremely great sex, but unprotected sex and I wasn't on the pill.

I made a mental note to stop by the pharmacy for a morning-after pill the second I had the chance. That was certainly the last thing either of us needed right now.

I dressed and splashed water on my face then combed through my hair with my fingers as best as I could to make myself presentable before leaving the sanctuary of the bathroom and doing my personal version of the walk of shame.

"But can you feel her freaking out?" the woman asked.

"Yes, Lily. I can feel her."

"Then she's the one," she said matter-of-factly. "Why fight it?"

"You mean, like you did?" Thomas challenged.

Lily snorted. "Babe, I'm right here sporting yet another one of your offspring. It all worked out just fine, as intended. It will for James and Katherine too."

"It's not the same," James argued. "She doesn't know anything about us, about me."

"Then tell her."

Thomas laughed. "It's that simple, is it, slugger?"

Lily looked up and caught me eavesdropping from the doorway.

"Oh, well, good morning. Come on and join us. Sorry," she said holding up a piece of bacon as she popped it into her mouth. "The baby couldn't wait."

Thomas rolled his eyes, but he was grinning.

I wasn't exactly sure what I'd walked in on. What had James meant when he said I didn't know anything about him? His words had cut like a sharp knife.

One thing was certain, I didn't belong here. Maybe the cult rumors were all true after all because it was evident there was something major he was keeping from me. Sure, they were all a little odd, but for the most part everyone I'd met from Collier seemed like good, decent people. What could be so bad that he couldn't just explain it to me?

"Um, I should probably get home."

"Have some breakfast and I'll drive you home."

Shit. I'd forgotten my car was still at the courthouse since I'd ridden with James.

"Okay," I conceded, feeling like he was leaving me with no option.

"Hi. I'm Lily Collier and this is my mate, Thomas," the blonde officially introduced herself.

I took the hand she offered and gave it a firm shake.

Mate. There was that word again.

"Husband," Thomas corrected. "I'm her husband."

Lily snorted and rolled her eyes. "Whatever," she muttered.

Maybe mate was just what they called their spouse within the cult. Except I wasn't James's spouse. Significant other, then?

I had the onset of a headache trying to figure it all out.

"Grab a plate and eat up. There's plenty," she insisted.

My eyes found James's. He smiled and nodded.

There was a mound of food on the counter, way more than any three or four people could possibly eat. I took a spoonful of scrambled eggs, a biscuit, and a couple pieces of bacon and sat in the open seat at the table stuck between James and Thomas, and across from Lily.

She looked at my plate and frowned. "Aren't you hungry? Damn, I thought for sure you would have worked up her appetite better than that," she said to James causing me to blush.

"Lily," Thomas warned.

"Nope. I am not responsible for what comes out of my mouth when you knock me up. Thems the rules, buster. Or have you forgotten?"

"As if you'd let me," he grumbled.

I had to bite back a chuckle.

There had always been something a little intimidating about Thomas, so seeing him interact with his wife, or mate, was certainly eye-opening.

Thomas and James got up to refill their plates heaping with food.

"Will they actually eat that much?" I asked Lily.

She scoffed. "That's only seconds."

I had never seen James eat like that. Where did he put it all? He was in excellent shape. If I'd had any question about that, it was laid to rest last night.

My cheeks burned once more as my mind drifted off to memories of a naked James.

"I know that look. Wow, James…"

He put his hand over her mouth to shut her up.

"Do something about this?"

Thomas chuckled. "As if I could."

"Ew. Lily! You licked me," James yelled as he jerked his hand away from her.

"Well, don't put your hand between my mouth and my food. Didn't your mother teach you anything? So, Katherine, tomorrow night I'm getting together with just a few friends. You should join us."

"No!" Thomas and James said in unison.

Lily rolled her eyes. "I just want to get to know her and what better way than a small girls' night in?"

"*No!*" they both repeated adamantly.

She huffed in frustration. "Fine. But you can't keep us apart forever," she grumbled. "How about lunch sometime soon?"

"Uh, sure," I said, suddenly curious and feeling just a bit defiant over the fact that James clearly didn't want me to be friends with her.

"Great."

James shot her a look.

"Come on, slugger. Time to go," Thomas said practically lifting her from her seat and pushing her towards the door.

"I'll call you later," Lily assured me with a wink.

James scrubbed his hands across his face as they left.

"You really don't want me to hang out with her, huh?"

"Trust me when I say absolutely nothing good will come from it."

Nothing good for me, or him?

I suddenly wanted to get to know Lily Collier very badly.

James
Chapter 11

Three days ago, after an extremely awkward encounter with Thomas and Lily, I'd driven Katherine home, kissed her goodbye, and hadn't seen or heard from her since, at least not as me.

I'd still been sneaking over each night to lie under her porch, so I knew she was fine, but we hadn't talked about it. I didn't know how she felt about what had happened between us and she hadn't asked to see me again.

I hadn't meant to let things go so far. I shouldn't have allowed it.

What had I been thinking?

The truth was, I hadn't been thinking at all. I'd allowed my animalistic urges to consume me, and I'd acted without thought of the consequences.

She was human and could just brush it off as a relapsed one-night stand with her ex and move on. But I wasn't human and she was supposed to be mine. That need to claim her was stronger than ever now and I didn't know how to stop it.

I knew I was going to have to go on full detox just to get a grip on the situation. I'd been here before after we'd broken up, but there had been little hope of fixing us back then. Katherine had made it clear it wasn't going to work.

This time it was different. She'd been so responsive to my touch and maybe even happy about it. That made it even harder to stay away from her.

I was starting to resent this stupid dog bed under her porch when I knew I could be wrapped up in her warmth in her bed instead.

That would be so easy, but where would that leave us? Still stuck.

If I told Katherine what I was, she'd fear me, and where would that leave the Pack? I'd taken an oath to protect them. How could I do that if I outed our secret to a human? And I didn't think I could actually live with her as man and wife in the human world while keeping this side of me to myself. I may have been willing to do that once upon a time when I'd been young and naïve, but now? I had too many ties and responsibilities to the Pack to just turn my back and walk away from them all.

I sighed and laid my head down on the stupid dog bed she'd left me. There was fresh water and some of her leftovers in the bowls she'd also brought for me. Thank God she was at least trying to feed me real food and not that nasty dogfood.

In many ways I felt like she was turning me into her pet and I equally resented and loved her for it.

The quiet of the night was broken by the crunch of tires on her gravel drive way. I wasn't certain of the time, but no one would be coming to her at this hour.

As I recognized the car, the hair on the back of my neck stood up and I let out a low growl, but then I heard something different–the soft cry of a baby.

A baby?

What was that asshole doing with a baby at Katherine's house at this hour of night?

I stayed put and fought my wolf to be quiet.

Allen, the asshole, walked up the front porch and knocked on the door. When there was no sound from within the house, he banged on the door a little louder.

"Katherine," he called out.

It felt like some time had passed and he was starting to walk back down the stairs when the door opened and her scent drifted down to me.

"Allen? What are you doing here?"

"I'm so sorry, but I'm not cut out for this. I'm on-call this week and there was an issue that required the immediate removal of this baby girl. She's already been processed through the clinic, but I can't find anyone to take her. I'm exhausted and she won't stop crying. I don't know what to do. I don't even have anything for her at my place. This isn't supposed to happen."

She sighed. "Do you have her paperwork with you?"

"Yes. It's in the car. I've called everyone on the list."

"Okay. Give her to me and go get her paperwork. I'll take her for the night and we'll try again for placement in the morning."

"Really?"

"Yeah. It doesn't happen often, but it does happen. Life outside the big city. I have everything here that I need for a night. It's fine."

Allen passed the baby to her and then ran back to his car.

"Hey there, sweet girl. Having a rough night?" Katherine lovingly cooed.

I could see her cuddling the infant to her chest through the slats in the porch. It hit me square in the chest.

My head was suddenly clouded with visions of her holding our child.

The reality of those visions made me sad and I held in the urge to let out a howl of mourning.

A half-breed child risked being snubbed by both the human and the shifter world. I would never knowingly do that to an innocent child.

Allen returned, had her sign something, and then handed her a folder and left without any issues. I was thankful for that.

"Okay, baby girl, let's get you settled down for the night."

They went inside, but I could hear her movements as she walked around getting things prepared for the baby.

That night I struggled to sleep as a dozen new thoughts and fears ran through my mind.

Katherine loved children and she would never be okay not having one of her own. Seeing her with the child made me realize that I wasn't selfish enough to do that to her.

It only reaffirmed my need to stay away from her and allow her to live her own life without the burden of me.

Once they were both soundly sleeping, I crept out from under the porch and ran home. The wind in my fur was normally a welcome comfort, but this time it was a sharp painful reminder of just how different we were.

I stopped and howled out my grief into the desolate darkness.

Knowing what I had to do, I ran straight home, shifted, and packed a bag. In some ways this would be easier done in my wolf, at least to start. So, I sat down and wrote out six letters, one to each of my friends and one group letter to my deputies.

I wasn't sure I could do this fully here, but I didn't really want to leave Collier, so it was a place to start. If it didn't work, I knew I would have to go away, probably to Westin Pack for a full rehab, or there was that shifter rehabilitation place up in Canada to consider. Tim Smith had great luck taming his wolf there.

Knowing there were options if this didn't work helped. But the thought of never seeing Katherine again hurt like a sonofabitch.

I decided at the last minute to just shift back and run over to the jailhouse in my fur. My wolf was angry at me and I didn't blame him in the least.

I'd never felt so alone and scared in my entire life, but I was resolute in my reasons. I was doing this to protect Katherine, to give her the life she deserved filled with love, happiness, a human life, and an armful of babies that I could never fully give her.

This was all for her no matter how badly it hurt me.

I shifted back to my skin to make it easier to get settled. I let myself into the building and went right to the cells. I had my keys with me, so I walked into one of them and set my bag down on the floor. I took out the six envelopes and lined them up in front of the door. They were all labeled to be clear who they went to.

Once settled, I gritted my teeth and nodded.

"This is the right thing to do," I assured myself before shifting to my fur and settling down on the bed.

We'd used the cells to dry out alcoholics and drug addicts in the past. I had no reason to suspect it wouldn't work for me too. Katherine was an addiction to me just as strong as any other. I would overcome it.

Mentally and physically exhausted, I drifted off to sleep only to be awoken a few hours later when my guys arrived for work.

"What the hell?" Ryder cursed.

"Is that the Sheriff?" Julian asked. "Sure looks like his wolf."

I jumped down and nudged the envelope to them with my nose so it slid right under the bars. He bent down and picked it up opening it quickly when he saw it was addressed to the team.

"Shit!"

"What is it?" Deaton asked.

"James found his true mate. He doesn't say who but for some reason thinks he can't have her and is trying to detox her out of his system. Boss, this is insane."

"What else?" Ryder asked.

"No matter what we can't let him out of the cell. His orders. Deaton, there's a whole page here to you, briefing you on the case he's working on."

Julian passed it to him.

Ryder shook his head and shot me an annoyed look.

"Everyone says find your true mate, but why? All it does is cause trouble. I hope I never find mine," he insisted.

In that moment, I understood exactly where he was coming from.

"Someone should call Thomas and let him know," Deaton advised.

"Fine, I'll do it," Julian said as he walked over to his desk and dialed the Alpha.

I went back to my cot and laid down, trying to tune them all out. Aside from feeling like I was drowning in a fishbowl, so far it wasn't so bad.

Within the hour Thomas, Clay, Wyatt, Austin, and Emmett were all standing before me reading the letters I'd wrote to each of them personally. I needed them to understand that this wasn't something they could just bail me out of. I had to do this myself.

"You're an idiot," Wyatt said.

"When did he meet his true mate? And why is he fighting it?" Clay asked.

"Because she's human," Emmett informed them.

"Yeah, it's Katherine," Thomas confirmed.

"He didn't mention that to me at all. Did he tell you guys that?" Austin asked.

"It's right here," Emmett said. "*I don't necessarily want this getting out, but I know you, without this knowledge you'll never just let me do this alone. This isn't like a normal situation. My true mate is a human and I cannot risk the safety and security of the Pack by accepting it, and I cannot live two separate lives by keeping her in the dark. So this is the way it has to be. Please respect that and support me.*" He looked up at me. "Dude, always. I'm team James no matter what."

"How long have you known, Thomas?" Wyatt asked.

"Maybe a week. Not long. Remember that day I came into Kate's to meet James and he was just sitting in the car and wouldn't get out?"

"Yeah, you went out to check on him and then the two of you drove off."

"That was the day he told me."

"I'm not surprised it's Katherine," Clay surprised me by saying. "It just makes sense."

"Katherine Carter, right? I knew he messed around with her a bit when we were younger and the few times I've seen them together there was definite chemistry, but he hasn't been with her for years. How the hell has he managed to fight a true mate bond all this time? And what changed?"

"He's been wolf stalking her nearly every night for a long time. Rarely sleeps in his own bed. They got thrown together on a case this week and I know for a fact that she ended up sleeping over. Lily and I brought breakfast to check on him and she was still there."

I growled and snapped at him.

"Don't get mad at me for it. This was your doing. And for the record, I would never keep true mates apart. I don't care that she's a human. We can deal with that part. I spent enough hours thinking Lily was leaving me and breaking our bond when we first found each other to know that I could never do that to someone. And we don't even know what she does or doesn't feel. This is new territory for me. So, no James, I will not honor your request, at least not now. If there's any chance whatsoever that she feels the bond too, then I can't do that to her. I just can't."

I whined and turned my back on him.

"What did he ask you?" Clay asked.

"He asked me to command him to forget her if things get bad and he can't do it on his own."

"You have to," Austin said. "If it gets that bad, you have to. This is James we're talking about."

"I'm not sure I can," Thomas said.

"Well, we don't need to worry about it just yet. Give him a few days in the tank to dry out and then we'll see what we're dealing with," Wyatt suggested. "A human? I honestly don't know how I would have handled it if Kate had been a human."

"If it were Winnie, I wouldn't care. She's mine, period," Clay insisted. But he didn't know how it felt, and he didn't have the position within the Pack to consider the way I did.

"I'll be by later to keep you company," Austin told me as they turned to leave.

I hated having their pity. I knew I was doing the right thing, not for me, but for her.

Katherine
Chapter 12

James was ghosting me. I couldn't even believe it. I should have seen it coming, but I hadn't, and it physically hurt knowing it. There was this desperation within me to go and knock some sense into him, but my stubborn pride was keeping me from doing it.

That wasn't entirely true. I'd take the hit to my pride and go after him, but I had a baby to consider. Rein had been passed off to me in the middle of the night and there was no one available to take her.

My team and I had been working around the clock trying to find a local placement for her. I didn't want to send her away, but our options were dwindling. In the meantime, I'd kept her.

The bags under my eyes were a sign of just how well that was going. I was exhausted. Babies were no joke and this one had colic and cried a lot. She always wanted to be held. My arms were finally starting to feel normal again and not like an overcooked noodle or sore like I'd decided to start bench pressing a gazillion pounds. How could one tiny baby be such a physical workout?

Days seemed to blur one into the other until I'd lost track of them.

There were a few things I had to do this week, like face my dad in court regarding the Collier boys' case. Mom had agreed to keep Rein for me while I was in court, but otherwise she had pretty much been with me nonstop since Allen dropped her off on my doorstep in the middle of the night.

I sent James another text just asking him to please update me on the results of the DNA test. I didn't want to go into it blindly, but it wasn't the first time I'd tried reaching out to him about it.

I got it. He regretted our little reunion while working on the case together. He couldn't possibly make that any more clear and it really pissed me off to think about it.

Being with him made me so happy, as if somehow a missing part of me had been found. Without him, I felt empty and hollow inside. I was snapping at everyone in the office and a very unpleasant person to be around overall. So much so, that it seemed like even the wolf had stopped coming around at night and I missed him.

Everyone around me was dismissing the shifts in my mood as experiencing normal temporary mom life with an infant, but there was nothing normal about how I was feeling.

A part of me felt like I was completely obsessed with him. I'd even dragged poor little Rein over to his house three times this week. His car was parked outside, but the house was always dark and he never answered when I banged on the door.

I even had to stop myself just short of actually breaking down his door.

I hated feeling like this. It was even worse than when I'd told him we needed to take a break and not rush things so quickly back when we were dating. I wasn't even sure how I'd survived that time in my life, but this was a million times worse.

My phone rang and I answered without even bothering to see who it was.

"Katherine Carter?"

"Speaking," I said as I juggled the baby in one arm while reaching for her pacifier with the other. "What can I do for you?"

"Hi, this is Deputy Deaton over in Collier County. I have the DNA results from the test you and Sheriff Blakely requested."

I grit my teeth and then blurted out, "He couldn't be bothered to call me with them himself?"

There was an uncomfortable pause on the other line before he cleared his throat.

"I'm sorry ma'am, but the Sheriff has taken a personal leave of absence and I've been reassigned to the case."

"And I'm just finding this out now? We're due in court this afternoon."

"Yes ma'am. The results just came through and I am packing up to head there now."

"Great, just great. Well, what were the results?"

"There was only one set of DNA found on the joint and it belongs to a Ronald Dixon, ma'am."

My heart skipped a beat. "Shit. The kids were telling the truth."

"It would appear so," Deaton confirmed. "Will CPS be testifying on behalf of the boys now or should I expect you'll be backing the DA?"

"Bring the full panel results to the courthouse. I'm leaving now and will try to catch up with Bucky to update him ahead of the trial. This changes everything. If he doesn't drop the case immediately, I'll have to speak to the boys to prepare them for this. So please have them arrive at least half an hour early."

"Yes, ma'am."

I hung up the phone with a heavy heart. James had taken leave because of me. I knew it had to be so. He'd already told me he wasn't exactly close with his family, so unless something happened with one of his Six Pack friends, then it had to be me. Why?

Didn't he know how badly I wanted to be with him?

No, you idiot, because you never bothered to tell him that.

I groaned thinking of what a mess I'd made of everything.

Opening my contacts, I scrolled through to find Lily Collier. After meeting her over breakfast the "night after," I had looked her up and added her to my phone contacts fully intending on following up with her about lunch sometime.

I'd changed my mind when the days following made it clear that James had wanted nothing more than a quick roll in the sheets.

A stabbing pain shot through me as I rubbed at my chest.

It had been so much more than that. Hadn't it?

Before I could chicken out, I hit the call button.

"Hello?"

"Um, hi, is this Lily?"

"Yes, who is calling?"

"Hi, uh, I guess I already said that. This is Katherine. Katherine Carter. We met at James Blakely's house last week."

"Oh, Katherine. Yes of course, how are you?"

"Good. Well, yeah, I'm fine. I just have a sort of odd question to ask you."

"Sure. Ask me anything."

"Is everything okay with the, uh, Six Pack? Like nothing bad happened to any of them, did it?"

"The Six Pack? No. Everyone's fine."

I sighed. "So it is me then. Thanks, Lily."

She started to protest in the background, but I quickly ended the call, loaded up Rein and headed over to my mother's.

"What is it, Katherine?" she asked me the second we walked through the door a few minutes later.

"What? Nothing. I'm fine."

"I'm your mother and I know when you are not fine, and right now you are very not fine."

I scoffed and frowned. "That doesn't even make sense. Look, I'm just tired and I don't have time to talk right now. I have to be in court in a few hours and I have some things to work out before that. Can you still watch the baby?"

"Yes, of course. I've blocked out the entire day for this little cutie."

She took the child, cooing and chatting at her in that ridiculous grandmotherly way. She might as well enjoy this kid, because the way I was masterfully screwing up my love life, I was going to end up a spinster.

I pressed a kiss to Rein's head and said goodbye. I couldn't get out of there fast enough.

Twice on the drive to the courthouse Lily called me. I chose to ignore it. James hadn't wanted me to spend time with her. He'd made that clear and I'd heard what I needed to hear from her already. There was nothing more for me to say or any reason to befriend her now.

I drove straight to Bucky's office. He looked flustered and confused when he saw me as he checked his watch.

"We're not due in court yet."

"I know, but we need to talk... now."

"Katherine, I have to prepare for court."

"Exactly."

"What does that mean?"

"Did Officer Dixon inform you of the fact that he was high during the altercation with the Collier boys?"

"What? No. He was on duty."

"Exactly."

"And you have proof of this?"

"I do."

"Shit."

"It gets worse."

"Give it to me."

"The boys are prepared to testify that Dixon turned off his car cam and got back out to confront them after they saw him smoking and called him out on it."

"Okay, so."

"He hit one of the boys, Bucky. Black eye and all. They were too scared to tell anyone, but the mother that picked them up will testify that her son did not have a black eye when she dropped the boys off and that he did have a swollen and later blackened eye when she picked them up. He assaulted a child."

"That's all the proof you have? A mother and some kids' testimony?"

"And the joint they picked up after he threw it at them. The boys were angry and they kept it. James had a full DNA panel run on it. Only one hit returned. A Ronald Dixon. What's Officer Dixon's first name?"

"Aw hell. You're serious?"

I nodded as he picked up the phone and yelled into it.

"Get Dixon in my office right now and I don't give a shit what he's doing."

Ten minutes passed before he burst through the doors. Clearly someone had let him know the true urgency of the situation.

I crossed my arms over my chest and glared at him but let Bucky take the lead.

"What's going on here? I was told this was an urgent matter."

"You struck a kid?"

"What are you talking about?"

The shocked look of guilt in his eyes told us both all we needed to know. That asshole had done it. He'd really done it.

"And you were high while on duty?"

"Is that what those punk kids said? They're liars. Delinquents."

"Two of them have never been in trouble a second of their life and the third, not for a long time. These are good kids," I insisted.

"I got them on vandalizing a public building."

"The movie theater is private property and Mr. Terrence dropped all charges against them."

"But the public misconduct charge will hold."

"Yeah, against you," Bucky said. "I'm dropping the case immediately."

"You'd believe the testimony of a couple of kids over an officer of the law? What kind of hick backwoods law do you practice here?"

"The legal kind," Bucky told him.

He picked up the phone and made a call.

"Judge Carter, the case against the three Collier minors is officially dropped. Yes, I have my reasons. Okay, we'll convene in your private chambers in twenty minutes. Katherine's here with me now. I don't know where James is, but I'll have my office track him down and let him know. Thanks."

"But..." Dixon protested.

Bucky raised a hand and glared at him.

"Don't. I don't have time for your games and personal vendettas. I've half a mind to make it damn certain you never work on the force again, but right now I have to go and clean up your mess. I won't blame the parents one bit if they decide to personally prosecute you for this. Actually, I think that's one case I'd be happy to take, so consider your next words *very* carefully."

Dixon was steaming as he turned and stormed out of the room, slamming the door behind him.

Bucky was unusually impressive as he sprang into action. Picking up the phone, he dialed another number.

"I need to speak with Sheriff Blakely immediately... Oh, I hadn't been informed. Who's his temporary replacement... Okay then, patch me through to Deputy Deaton..."

I listened in as he relayed the update and then looked down at his watch.

"Yeah. I'll see you in a few."

Hanging up the phone he turned his attention back to me.

"Come on. The Judge wants us all in his office in ten."

We were a united force entering my dad's chambers. It wasn't often that the DA and defense were in agreement on a case like this.

"What's this all about?" Dad asked.

Bucky and Deaton just looked at each other.

I rolled my eyes and sighed.

"New evidence has been brought to the case and there was a lot more to it than originally described."

I told him about my follow up with the boys and how James and I had uncovered the rest of the story. I told him all about the joint, the camera being turned off, and the black eye. I explained how we'd acquired the information and the marijuana in question plus the DNA results that confirmed all suspicions.

"Those city cops think they can just come down here and get away with murder. I have half a mind to toss his ass in jail for this. Are the boys okay?"

"They're obviously shaken up by this experience, but they're good kids from good families and they'll get through this. My office is prepared to offer any support and therapy they may need."

"And where is James?" he inquired.

Deaton cut his eyes towards me and then cleared his throat. "He's taking some personal leave, sir."

That was all the confirmation I needed. James was absolutely avoiding me, and it made some part of me deep inside snap in total fury.

Somehow, I managed to hold it all together as we wrapped up the meeting.

Dad closed the hearing to the public as the boys were informed of the change and that all charges were being dropped. Nothing would be on their record.

Dixon didn't bother to show up, but with Dad's encouragement, Bucky lined up an arrest warrant for him. There was still some uncertainty with the boys over testifying against him, but the process was in place. At the very least he'd face disciplinary action.

We were all committed to ensuring no other kid was harmed by him again.

Feeling exhausted, I went to pick up Rein.

Halfway to my mom's house, Allen called me.

"Hey, hey. I have good news."

"Tell me, because I could seriously use some good news right about now."

"I have a commitment to take Rein off your hands. In fact, I'm on my way to your house now to get her."

I shouldn't have felt as relieved as I did, but for the first time all day a smile broke out across my face.

"Thanks, Allen. She's actually at my parents' house since I had court today. Can you just meet me there?"

"You got it. I'm on my way. Oh, and how did the case go?"

"All charges against the boys were dropped. I'll fill you in on the rest later."

"That's great news."

He started talking to tell me about the family the baby would be moved to. We were still on the phone as we both simultaneously arrived at the house.

Allen didn't linger as he had places to be. He signed for custody of Rein, gathered up her things, and just like that, she was gone.

"You look exhausted, sweetheart. How about a nice meal and then an early night?"

"I'm going to pass on the food, but thanks. Wine and a bubble bath sound like a better alternative. Having a baby sure is hard work."

She shook her head. "It's not easy to care for someone else's child, but when it's your own... okay, it's still a lot of work, but the most fulfilling and rewarding job you'll ever have."

She grabbed me by the neck and pulled me down to kiss my cheek.

"Nothing is greater than being your mom."

"Love you too, Mom."

James
Chapter 13

Days and nights blurred together as one. I could have been in there for years for all I knew. The only thing I was certain of was that this feeling of needing Katherine wasn't going away. If anything, it was getting worse.

My wolf and I were at odds, fighting an internal struggle for power.

The guys had been great. My deputies made sure I had plenty of meals and fresh water. They kept me informed on everything that was happening and Deaton had filled me in on the court case Katherine and I had been working together on.

He was sure to let me know how disappointed she was that I hadn't attended the final hearing. The guilt of that still weighed heavily on me.

What was I doing?

I didn't just want my mate… I needed her. She hadn't done or said anything for me to believe she would reject me, yet I was still terrified of trying to explain everything to her, and for the impact that could have on the Pack.

This wasn't just about me.

I wanted to protect her from the knowledge that there were beasts like me roaming around her town. The way Hollywood portrayed us would be the only thing she'd have to go by, and that wasn't going to help encourage her to keep an open mind.

We were the things nightmares were made of as far as humans were concerned, mythical creatures that they didn't even want to believe existed.

Of course, I knew that was comically different from my reality. Yes, wolf shifters could go wild. Lone wolves in particular could be a danger, but no more so than a human serial killer. Not all humans were dangerous and not all shifters were either.

I desperately wanted to prove that to her, but with no way to know for sure how she would take it, I just couldn't risk it.

"Where is he?"

"Lily, Pack Mother, you aren't allowed back here," Ryder protested.

"Move out of my way."

She looked around and spotted me in the cell. Frowning, she pursed her lips and shook her head as she walked deliberately towards me.

"What the hell are you doing? I'll tell you what. You're making yourself miserable and you're making Katherine miserable too. I know she's human, and I can't pretend to know what she's going through, but I know the sound of an upset woman when I hear it."

I shifted immediately and lunged forward to grab hold of the bars.

"You talked to her?"

"Yeah, about a week ago. Thomas kept telling me to stay out of it, but I can't stand to see you like this, James. I've got a whole team researching human shifter relationships right now as well as how to break a true mate bond."

It felt like a knife slicing open my heart to even think of breaking my bond to her.

"What did you find?" I asked, like some sort of masochist hellbent on destroying himself.

"Well, I don't think the whole human shifter mating match is all that new or uncommon. Okay, it's not something you hear about every day, but there have been documented cases all throughout history."

"But that doesn't change my circumstances here."

"And what is that?"

"Lily, I swore an oath to Thomas, to the Pack. How can I ever explain to Katherine what I am without breaking that promise and exposing us all?"

"But if she's your true mate…"

"There's no guarantee she's going to handle that and keep our secrets just because she's my mate."

"Oh James. You really are an idiot. Just talk to her."

"You don't know how badly I wish I could."

Lily was seconds away from telling me how ridiculous I was being when Austin and Emmett walked in.

"Lily, what are you doing here?"

"Telling this fool what a complete moron he's being."

"Oh, well, carry on then. We'll wait for our turn next," Austin said.

"What do you guys want?"

"At least you're out of your fur. But man, you reek. Dude, take a break from this shit and take a damn shower," Emmett insisted.

I glared at him.

"Look, we made some…" Austin started but Emmett punched him to shut him up as the two of them shared a look.

Lily turned to them and put her hand on her hip.

"Spill it, now. What have you come up with?"

Emmett glared at Austin daring him to speak again.

Austin's face turned red all the way to the tips of his ears.

"Okay, okay! We called in some favors and got a dose of memory serum."

"What?" Lily screeched. "How?"

"It doesn't matter. The point is, you can tell Katherine now, and if it goes badly, then we'll just erase all mention of it for her."

I growled.

"You aren't wiping my mate's memories, you idiots."

"Well…" Lily started as she shot me an apologetic look and shrugged. "I mean it's not the worst idea they've ever had. This could work, James. If all goes well and she doesn't entirely freak out then you're in the clear. No more self-punishment or detox or whatever the hell this is all about. You can get on with your life one way or another."

"And then what? Say she freaks out and we use the serum. Where does that leave me? I still don't know how to break this bond with her and, quite frankly, I don't want to."

"Fine, then I'll sweet talk Thomas into interceding if we have to use the serum on her. He can't break the bond for you, but he can make you forget it."

"Don't you think others would have tried that before if it was that simple?"

"I don't know. I'm trying here, okay. You'd likely always feel like this part of you is missing, you just wouldn't know who or what," she blurted out. "Trust me, I thought long and hard about this, too, during my mating days."

"You didn't want Thomas?" Austin asked.

"No. He's, well, Thomas! I was devastated when I found out he was my true mate."

"Does he know this?" Emmett asked,

"Of course he does. How are *you* just now hearing about it?" They both shrugged.

"When we first met you, it was just obvious that you were into each other," Austin insisted.

Both guys looked at me and all I could do was shrug.

Thomas and I were close, and he had confided all of it to me.

"Asshole. You knew?"

"They made it. They're fine. The bond just makes you crazy. Someday you'll understand."

"Crazy, like locking yourself into a jail cell in hopes of detoxing like a freaking addict?" Emmett asked.

"Exactly!"

Lily's face cracked.

I glared at her.

"Don't," I warned.

But it was too late. She burst out laughing to the point that tears were running down her cheeks. Austin and Emmett quickly joined her.

"Sure, laugh it up."

"Come on, it's kind of funny," Austin insisted.

"You're assholes. All three of you."

Thomas walked in and growled.

"Did you just call my mate an asshole?"

"Yes, especially her."

Lily stopped him when he lunged for me.

Admittedly, pissing off the Alpha was probably not my smartest move.

"Don't. It's fine," she said, holding her belly as she laughed.

Suddenly she stilled and her eyes widened.

"Dammit, James. You made me pee myself."

Without another word, she waddled off towards the bathroom.

Thomas just shook his head watching her go.

"What are you doing here?" Emmett asked him.

"What are *you* doing here?" Thomas countered.

"Trying to spring him."

"Yeah, we have a plan," Austin admitted.

"It's the dumbest plan ever. I'm not doing it."

"Tell me."

Austin filled him in and, much to my horror, Thomas agreed with him.

"You're really doing this because of the oath you took when you became Sheriff?" he asked.

"Yes. I have responsibilities that supersede myself."

"No," Thomas said. "We cherish and protect true mates in this Pack. It's just as important as risking exposure. If that's what this is all about then I command you to get your ass out of that cage and go talk to your mate once and for all."

When I didn't make any move to leave, Thomas barked an order to Ryder.

"Get him out of here. Now!"

"Yes, sir," my deputy said, scrambling to unlock the cell.

"This is a mistake. I'm not ready."

"And you're never going to be, so just man up and do what you have to do."

Shaking my head, I grabbed my things not even bothering to dress and walked outside. The bright sun burned my eyes as I tried to retreat back inside only to find a wall of muscle shoving me forward.

"You heard the Alpha," Emmett insisted.

"Dammit, I hate you guys."

"Hate's a pretty strong word, but in this instance, we're going to ignore it and chalk it up to mating insanity," Austin teased.

I shifted, growled at them and then picked up my bag in my teeth and ran all the way home.

When I shifted back and let myself into the house, I realized Emmett was right. I really did stink.

Dropping my stuff on the kitchen table, I walked straight back to the shower.

By the time I was clean and freshly dressed, Clay and Wyatt were sitting at my kitchen table.

"What are you assholes doing here?"

"Heard we missed the show and wanted to stop by and see how you're doing," Clay said,

"Look, we've been there, James. We know what you're going through," Wyatt tried to explain.

"Your mates aren't human. You don't know what I'm dealing with here."

Clay shrugged. "Mating's mating. It all makes you a little crazy."

"Yeah, I heard Michael from Westin Force literally kidnapped his woman during his mating call recently. Doesn't matter who she is, if she's yours, then we get it. Nothing will stop you from wanting her. You don't really have a choice in this, so just do the right thing and claim her already. She'll come around," Wyatt insisted,

"You can't possibly know that for sure."

"Well, there's only one way to find out," Clay said, tossing me my cell phone.

"I haven't even seen her in a week. I'm not just going to pick up the phone and call her now."

"Two weeks, or two and a half, I guess."

"What?"

"Yeah, it's been two weeks since you checked yourself into rehab or whatever we're calling it," Wyatt explained.

"Two weeks?"

I ran a hand through my hair. I had no idea that much time had passed. I couldn't exactly keep track of days and nights when I couldn't even see outside from the cell I was in. At first, I counted based on when the guys came and went, but after a while that all seemed to blur into one continuous nightmare.

"Okay, so we see you're going to need a little time to process this. Try to get a good night's sleep and we'll be back in the morning to check on you, okay?" Clay offered.

"Yeah, sure. Thanks. It's really been two weeks?"

"Yes, James. You've been pathetically wallowing in self-pity for two freaking weeks. Now it's time to grow up and put those big boy pants back on."

"Wyatt's right. You can't hide from this forever. You have to deal with it."

I sighed, feeling completely deflated.

After Katherine had broken up with me the first time, I'd battled severe depression. I knew the bottom of the dark hole I now found myself in. That was the thing I wanted to overcome.

A good night's sleep in a real bed was a nice start.

Tomorrow, I'd deal with it. One way or another, something had to give.

Katherine
Chapter 14

I was back to throwing myself into my work, feeling numb and trying to stave off depression. James hadn't gotten back to me, not once. A part of me was terrified something bad had happened to him, but over the last few weeks I'd crossed paths with people who knew him and they had assured me he was fine and just dealing with some personal stuff.

The fact that this personal stuff seemed to occur right after we'd made love and spent the night in each other's arms was hard to swallow. I knew it had to be related. I'd seen the looks and understood the careful phrasing they used when speaking to me. But I wasn't the one who had hurt him. He had hurt me.

Maybe I deserved it. Maybe it had all just been payback for the way I'd dumped him all those years ago. I expected more from James, but maybe I'd been wrong about him.

Just the thought sent a sharp piercing pain through my chest.

That was happening pretty regularly, mostly when I let myself think about him. I'd even gone to the doctor to have it checked out, just to make sure I wasn't battling heart disease or had a stroke or something. She hadn't found anything physically wrong with me.

Today was another Saturday, a day I come to dread. I didn't have work to bury myself in. There was nothing pressing for me to do. Last week I'd purged and painted the spare bedroom. The week before that, I had sanded and stained the front porch. It was then that I realized my wolf had stopped coming to visit me, too. I was truly and utterly alone.

My anxiety was stronger than ever and the change to my meds, that I was now taking daily instead of as needed, wasn't really helping.

The worst part of all is that when I was alone in the quiet with my thoughts, I always thought of him. It was the worst kind of obsession.

"Not today, Katherine," I said aloud. "Today, I'm getting up and getting out of here. I will not wallow any longer."

With that bit of a pep talk, I forced myself into the shower, dressed for the day, and then opened my fridge to grab a bite to eat. There was nothing there that would be considered edible any longer.

"Guess I'm going to the grocery store."

Fully aware I was talking to myself, I grabbed my purse and left the house.

Powell's was only a few minutes' drive away. It was a larger local grocery store that specialized in local produce and goods. I always preferred to support local businesses when I could and hands-down, they had the best options around.

I snagged a loose cart on my way to the door and tried to put a smile on my face knowing it would be a miracle if I got through this trip without running into someone I knew.

Not five steps inside and one of my mother's church friends yelled out my name and waved from the check out.

I gave a quick wave and turned away from her, not wanting to encourage a conversation.

I grabbed some fresh fruit and enough vegetables for a small salad before hitting the aisles. I walked up and down, covering each one of them regardless of whether I needed anything from them or not. I had no list and was just picking up whatever I saw of interest.

I stopped and bought some meat from the butcher case, apologizing and telling him I was in a hurry when he tried to make small talk with me.

And when I saw another one of Mom's church lady friends up ahead, I ducked down another aisle in avoidance to find myself standing in front of shelves full of pads and tampons.

I froze as I stared at them.

When had I last bought them?

Hell, when had I last used them?

My mouth dropped open and I grabbed for my phone to pull out the calendar. I was usually good about tracking such things, but lately I'd been in such a funk that I hadn't even thought about it.

I scrolled back... seven weeks.

Seven weeks!

I started to hyperventilate. My chest was getting tighter by the second as I tried to count back the days to when I'd had sex with James.

We hadn't used protection.

I had fully intended to pick up a morning after pill just to be safe.

Allen had dropped baby Rein off at my house.

I'd never made it to the pharmacy.

The edges of my vision were beginning to darken as I leaned over my cart in hopes that it would keep me upright.

I couldn't be pregnant. James didn't want me. I was certain he wouldn't want a kid with me. We'd be tied together for at least the next eighteen years.

This cannot be happening!

Looking around, I saw the pregnancy tests next to the feminine products and further down the aisle were all baby products. What the hell? I'd be willing to bet the freaking condoms were around here somewhere too.

Someone at this store had a very sick sense of humor.

My hand reached out to grab a pregnancy test when someone called my name.

"Katherine? Is that you?"

I dropped that box and jerked my hand back like it had just burned me.

Anxiously, I looked up to see Lily freaking Collier headed my way.

She smiled, then her face morphed into concern as she looked at me and then down to the floor and back to me again with wider eyes.

"Um, did you drop this?"

"No," I said a little too fast. "It's not mine."

Without another word, I abandoned my cart and turned to walk away.

"Katherine, stop. Please."

I froze and turned slowly, not wanting to face her.

"Can we go somewhere and talk? You look like you could use a friend right about now."

Hers words cracked through my hardened shell as tears welled up in my eyes and I nodded my head.

"You can come back to my place if you want, but I'd bet yours is closer."

She seemed to understand that now was not the time for a public breakdown.

"Okay."

"Go wait in your car and I'll check out. I'll just be a minute and then I'll follow you home, okay?"

I nodded, not sure what else to do. I needed someone to talk to more than ever. I didn't know her, but that didn't seem to matter.

Practically running from the store, I sat in my car crying as I waited.

True to her word, Lily wasn't long before she tapped on my window and pointed out her car.

"I'll just follow you, okay?"

I nodded, unable to formulate any words.

As soon as she had her groceries loaded in the back of her mini-van, I pulled out and made sure I didn't go too fast or lose her along the way.

She pulled into my driveway right behind me.

"I have a few cold things here. Is it okay if I store them in your fridge while we talk?"

"Sure," I said.

She carried in more than I expected but as she started to unpack I realized most of it was mine.

"You bought my groceries?"

Lily shrugged. "I didn't want them to go to waste."

"Um, thanks."

"Wanna talk about this?" she asked, pulling the pregnancy test out of the last bag.

I burst into tears when I saw it.

She didn't say a word as she wrapped her arms around me and held me tight despite her protruding pregnant belly between us.

"It's going to be okay."

"It's not. He hates me."

"He doesn't hate you."

"You can't know that. He hasn't returned my calls or text. He won't answer his door. He even sent someone else in his place to cover the case we were working together. He is going out of his way to ghost me."

"He's an idiot."

I sniffed and pulled back, wiping my tears away.

"You can't tell him about this. It's probably nothing. I mean I can't be pregnant. We only had sex once."

"Did he use a condom?"

"No."

"Are you on birth control?"

"No."

"Then honey, it's possible."

She picked up the test and held it out to me.

"Only one way to know for sure."

I sniffled once more and nodded.

"Will you stay with me?"

She smiled with tears filling her own eyes.

"I'm not going anywhere."

"Okay."

I took the test and went to the bathroom. Opening the box, I read every word of the instructions. I knew I was partly stalling, but I also didn't want to mess it up or cause a false positive or something.

Finally, I opened the stick, pushed down my pants, and squatted over the toilet to pee on that damn thing.

"I'm not pregnant," I said.

"Keep telling yourself that," Lily yelled from the living room.

How the hell had she even heard me.

"I'm not pregnant," I said again. "I am not pregnant."

I cleaned up and took the test down the hall.

"How long does it say to wait? Because I know you read all the instructions first."

I glared at her. "Two minutes."

Lily pulled out her phone and set a timer.

"Now relax and just breathe."

"Easy for you to say. You're already knocked up."

"Honey, you may be too."

"Gah! Don't say that."

I took to pacing back and forth across the living floor, but when that alarm sounded on her phone, I froze.

"Do you want me to check it?"

"No. Yes. I don't know."

She picked it up and handed it to me.

"Whatever it says, it's going to be fine."

With shaky hands I took the test from her and slowly looked down.

My whole world fell apart in an instant.

"Positive," I whispered as I stared at two little pink lines.

I sat down hard and passed it to her.

"No doubt about that one, but if you want me to run out and buy a dozen more just to be sure, I can. Trust me, I've been there."

I shook my head feeling an odd calm wash over me.

"No. It won't change anything. I'm almost three weeks late. I think I already knew and clearly you can't just manifest away something you've already created. Lord knows I tried."

She snorted but stood up and moved to sit next to me.

When she wrapped an arm around my shoulders, I leaned into her comfort and rested my head on her shoulder.

"I never in a million years thought I would end up a single mother."

Lily scoffed. "Girl, you will not be going through this alone."

"That's nice of you to say, but that's truly my reality."

"It is James's baby, right?"

"There's no one else," I confirmed.

"This will crack his stubborn ass for sure. When he finds out, nothing will stop him from getting to you and your child."

I shook my head and sat back to look in her eyes.

"Lily, you can't tell him. James has made it painfully clear how he feels about me. I'm not about to trap him out of pity or unnecessary responsibility. I'm perfectly capable of raising a child on my own."

She shook her head. "Not his child."

"What does that mean?"

"Look, there are things you don't know. Things he should have told you. He has his reasons for keeping his distance but *none* of them include not wanting to be with you. Everything he's done is to protect you."

"You're wrong," I insisted. "I made a mistake by letting him back in. It had felt so right, like I had no choice in the matter. I wanted to believe it was just fate, you know? Like we were meant to be together."

Her jaw dropped open in surprise.

"Is that what it feels like for you?" she blurted out.

"Excuse me?"

"I know I'm being weird right now, but honestly, you can tell me. What do you feel for James, Katherine?"

"I don't want to talk about it," I said.

"It's important, please?"

I shook my head. "It's my problem, not his."

"I think you're wrong about that. Tell me."

I started to tell her off, to ask her to leave, but when my mouth opened, everything spilled out of it.

"I feel this connection to him, Lily. It's so strong at times that it's like I can't even breathe when he's not around. And when he is, it just sort of feels as though my whole world righted itself. Without him, a part of me is missing. Always has been. I only feel completely myself when he's around, though sometimes I'm comforted by the wolf that lives under my porch too. I know, I sound insane. It's an obsession and I don't blame him for running away from me. If the tables were turned, I'd freak out and run away from him too. When we broke up several years ago it was bad. It took me a long time and a great deal of therapy and anxiety meds to get through it. But I survived it and learned to cope. Our paths don't cross often, so it's been bearable, but since we were together this last time, it's just gotten worse. So much worse."

"How so?"

"I've stalked him, Lily. Literally parked my car down the street and sat outside his house watching for him. He hasn't been there. I don't know how he knows, but he must, because he's not even coming home at night."

I expected her to freak out or tell me I was insane, maybe even call the police to report me or something. What I didn't expect was for her to laugh so hard that she grabbed her belly, cursed me, and waddled down the hall to my bathroom laughing the entire way.

Sitting there alone, I picked up the test once more and looked at it. My hand went to my stomach and rubbed it in a soothing circle.

"I'm sorry, baby. It's just going to be me and you from now on."

James

Chapter 15

I was trying to get my life back in order. There was certainly a lot to catch up on, but my constant thoughts were still on Katherine.

I had to know she was okay.

Late Saturday night, I stripped off my clothes, shifted, and ran to her house the way I had done so many times for so many years. I'd just keep my distance. She didn't even need to know I was there.

When I arrived and crept under the porch, I could hear laughter inside and soon Lily walked out of her house.

The two of them embraced.

"Call me if you need absolutely anything. I'm serious."

"I will. And thanks for everything today."

"Anytime."

Katherine stood there and watched Lily go before turning around. She gasped when she caught sight of me.

"You're back!"

I was startled she had even noticed, though I suppose with no one around to eat her leftovers my absence may have been noticeable.

My wolf's curiosity had him running towards her before I could stop him.

Cut it out, I urged him.

Mine! he insisted.

Katherine should have been terrified of my large wolf barreling towards her, but then his tongue was hanging out the side of his mouth and his tail was wagging behind him.

Instead of fear, she seemed happy to see my wolf. So much so that she dropped to her knees and wrapped her arms around me fisting her hands in my fur as she started to sob.

I sat back on my hindlegs and then lifted one large paw around her back to embrace her as best as I could in this form. We just sat there like that while she cried.

After a while she sat back on the bottom step of her porch and dabbed at her eyes.

"I'm sorry. I've just missed you so much and you have no idea how badly I needed you here today."

I whimpered trying to encourage her to keep talking.

Was she hurt?

Why was she so upset?

I had to know more.

I leaned my big head down and nudged her gently.

She started to pet me like a freaking dog, but I didn't care.

"Man, my life has been a mess since you took off. I never even got to tell you about James. It doesn't really matter now, I suppose. He's ghosted me."

No, I haven't. I'm right here, I wanted to say, but it only came out as a soft whine.

"It's probably for the best. He's made it painfully clear that he doesn't feel the same way about me as I feel about him."

What? What are you talking about?

"He's been my world for so long, even when we were apart, and being with him was everything to me. It was like magic, and for a moment I honestly thought there was hope for us. That was squashed quickly."

My head tilted to the side.

"Yeah, it wasn't pretty. You sleep with the only man you'll ever love and think your whole world was just made right only to have him go AWOL the next day and never hear from him again. Want to know a secret?"

I whined again and laid my head in her lap.

"He's the one for me. I don't know how to explain it, but it feels so much bigger than just me. It's like I was made for him and he for me, but obviously I'm just insane because he doesn't feel that way about me at all. I'm completely obsessed with a man who wants nothing more than a quick roll in the sheets."

She patted my head again but kept talking.

"I feel like such a fool, but I don't know how to break this hold he has over my heart. Maybe it's wrong, maybe I shouldn't be happy about it, but at least now I'll always have a small part of him with me. You see, I'm pregnant."

Pregnant?

My head started to spin. Katherine was pregnant?

"I just found out and I should be terrified about it, but I don't know. Maybe I'm just in shock. This certainly isn't how I ever had imagined it happening, but here it is. I'm going to have a baby."

She started to cry again and I couldn't shift fast enough.

"You're pregnant?"

Katherine stared at me in shock, then she screamed and stumbled backwards. I moved quickly to catch her as she fell. Her eyes were wide and half-crazed, not that I could blame her, but then she just fainted.

"Shit!"

I'd just shifted in front of a human. It didn't matter that she was my human, that was a huge do not do in the shifter world.

I looked around to ensure no one else saw me, even though I knew she had no neighbors nearby and I hadn't heard any cars approaching.

Pregnant? Katherine was pregnant.

I was going to be a father.

The whole world started to spin around me.

I pushed that aside and picked her up as I carefully carried her back inside and took her back to her bedroom to lay her down.

She was just in shock. I couldn't blame her. I was too. But I was also standing there naked. That wasn't going to help this situation any.

I started looking around for something to put on—a robe, sweatpants, anything.

Going through her drawers I realized everything was still so familiar, like she hadn't changed a thing over the years.

I froze when I opened the bottom drawer, my drawer. My clothes were still neatly folded there as if I'd never left. I pulled out a pair of sweats and a T-shirt to throw on, unable to believe she'd kept all of my stuff.

Was it that she felt our bond more than I imagined possible? Why else would she keep my things? It made my head swim thinking about it.

Only leaving her side long enough to go to the kitchen and get a soda, I returned and sat down on the bed next to her.

"Babe, I need you to open your eyes. I know you're freaked out, but I have to know you're okay," I said softly.

She moaned and her eyes fluttered open.

"James?"

"I'm here."

She groaned holding her head.

"I had the weirdest dream."

It would have been so easy to let her believe that, but I couldn't. If a baby was involved now then that changed everything.

That child would be a half-breed and that meant facing all sorts of obstacles that my human mate needed to know about.

"It's not a dream, babe. Now sit up and take a sip of this."

"Not a dream?"

"No, it's not. We have a lot to talk about."

"The wolf…"

"Was me. It was always me."

She sat up quickly and my gut wrenched at the look of fear in her eyes, but she took the soda I offered and sipped. I could see the wheels of her mind whirling.

"The wolf started coming around shortly after we broke up. I saw him off and on."

I nodded.

"That was you?"

"It was always me," I repeated.

"Why?"

That was a question I wasn't ready to answer.

"When did you find out you're pregnant?" I asked, deflecting her question.

She frowned. "Today. If you're asking if it's yours, there hasn't been anyone else."

"I know," I said softly.

"How is this possible?"

"I don't know. I'm sorry. I should have used protection. I just got so caught up in the moment that I didn't think."

"I don't mean about the baby. H-how are you, you know, a wolf? I saw you. I'm not crazy. One second you were standing there as a dog listening to me ramble on and the next you were, you, only naked. Oh my God, you were naked. Why? Where did you get those clothes? Oh my God, I'm going crazy, aren't I?"

"I found the clothes in my drawer," I told her honestly with a slight smirk. "Why do you still have my clothes in my drawer?"

I had to know. Even knowing that it didn't really matter, it still seemed important to me.

She blushed and pulled her knees up to her chest as she hid her face behind them.

"I kept it all," she whispered.

"What?"

"I kept it all, okay? I mean if that was really you outside then it shouldn't be some sort of shocker here. I already confessed that I have a slightly unhealthy obsession with you," she blurted out.

My chest constricted and I felt warm all over.

"You feel it too," I said reverently.

"Feel what?"

"Our bond."

She shook her head. "I don't even know what you're talking about. Are you going to explain to me how you were an animal one second and a man the next? Because I really think I must have hit my head or something. This can't be real."

"It's real," I assured her. "I can show you again if you'd like."

She shook her head. "No. Not yet. I'm a little freaked out and trying to come to terms with this."

I sighed. "I know. It's why I tried so hard to protect you from this."

"What?"

"Humans aren't supposed to know about this, about me. You're different."

She frowned. "How am I different?"

I looked into her eyes unable to stop myself.

"Because you're mine."

My heart raced waiting for her reaction, but when she burst out laughing and rolled her eyes, I scowled.

"That's the dumbest thing you've ever told me, and you just told me you're really a wolf."

"Katherine, you are mine. We are fated to be together."

She stopped laughing and glared at me. The fire in her eyes surprised me.

"If that were true, where the *hell* have you been? You won't answer my calls. You ignore my texts. Hell, you won't even answer your door when I practically knock it down. If we are so destined to be together, where the hell have you been and why would you just leave me alone to deal with all of this by myself?"

She started to cry again so hysterically that she began to hiccup.

I reached out to pull her into my arms, but she pushed me away.

It hurt to see her like this.

I tried again and this time she grabbed hold of my shirt and held tight as I wrapped my arms around her.

"I'm so sorry," I whispered. "I just wanted to protect you from all of this, from me. I didn't know you were suffering too."

"You can't protect me from this."

"I see that now."

For a long while neither of us spoke again as we just laid there holding each other. After a while her sobs turned to soft tears that morphed into light snores.

I kissed her forehead feeling more at peace than I'd ever felt before.

Careful not to wake her, I stretched her out on the bed and snuggled up next to her. My hand went to her still flat stomach.

A baby. We were going to have a baby.

Everything I'd put myself through, no both of us through, to protect her from this was for naught, because there was nothing on this Earth that would keep me from her now. I'd lived most of my life with only her in mind. I'd done what I thought I had to do no matter how miserable that made me. This changed everything.

Feeling more content than I could ever remember, I laid there watching her sleep until I drifted off into a deep slumber that I'd denied myself for weeks.

*****

"James? What are you doing here?" she asked as I stirred awake.

"Huh?"

I opened my eyes to see Katherine staring down at my hand still protectively on her stomach.

"Oh," she said softly. "It was real."

"I know this is a lot to take in, Katherine, and you have no reason whatsoever to trust me after the way I've behaved, but I promise you, I'm not going anywhere this time, not now, not ever."

She took a deep breath and let it out.

"James, I love you. That's never changed, but I don't want you to be here out of some unfounded obligation with this baby. You made it clear you didn't want to be with me after we sort of rekindled things, so let's not jump ahead into promises you can't keep. Okay?"

Her words sliced through me as I shook my head.

"You don't understand. It's not that I don't want to be with you, Katherine. Hell, I can't stay away from you. Trust me, I tried. Do you want to know where I've been since the last time we were together? Do you really want to know?"

She shook her head, but she said, "Yes."

"Are you sure you really want the whole ugly truth of it all?"

"I need to know. Everything. I still can't wrap my head around the fact that you were just morphed out of a wolf like something in the movies. It doesn't feel real, but I need to know."

"I was locked up in jail."

"What?"

"I just got out yesterday. I didn't even last twenty-four hours, and I had to see you. I needed to know you were okay. I didn't mean for you to see me and I sure as hell didn't mean to shift in front of you. I was just in shock when you said you were pregnant."

"Jail? What did you do?"

"It's not what you think. I did it to myself."

"But why would you do that? That's ridiculous."

"Maybe. There's a lot about me that you don't know and I'm not even sure you can truly understand."

"Because you're a werewolf? Wait, why were you a wolf in the daylight? It's not even a full moon."

I barked out a laugh and started to relax a little.

"I'm not a werewolf like you see in the movies. I don't shift with the full moon, well, not unless I choose to. You need to know that I'm not a monster and I would never hurt you."

She gave me a comical look and then her eyes widened.

"I know. I've never once thought to be afraid of you, not as a wolf and certainly not as a man. God, someone's going to commit me for even talking this way. None of this can be real. It just can't. You're punking me here, right?"

She looked around as if she was waiting for someone to jump out and yell, "Gotcha!"

Unfortunately, that wasn't going to happen. I'd made the jump, whether I'd meant to or not, and there was no turning back. Even if she chose not to have me in her life or my child's, she still needed to know in order to prepare him or her for a future most would never know or understand.

"Katherine, it's real. I'm real."

"If you aren't a werewolf, then what are you?"

"A wolf shifter."

"Wolf shifter," she repeated, rolling it around on her tongue. "And how is that different from a werewolf?"

I groaned. "Let me count the ways." With a chuckle I began trying to explain things to her. "First, my human side controls my inner beast. When I'm in my fur, it's largely still me."

"Like you hear and understand everything?"

"Everything," I assured her.

She blushed furiously, no doubt thinking back on all the things she'd confided in me recently. I wasn't even sure if she realized I had been around before, but something she said made me wonder if maybe she'd been more aware of my wolf than I'd suspected.

"Katherine, when did you first know my wolf was guarding you?"

She bit her lip and shrugged.

"I mean…" she paused and then groaned. "Okay, this is all weird and unbelievable, so why should this be any different? Ugh! Okay, so at first, I didn't know it was your wolf, though I've seen him a few times throughout the years. I just figured, you know, I live in the country and that means wild animals and all. He never threatened me, so I never worried about it."

She nibbled on her bottom lip and I knew there was more she wasn't saying.

"But…"

"I always knew he, or I guess you, were out there."

"That's not possible," I whispered to myself.

"See, I told you it was weird and you wouldn't believe me."

"No, sorry, continue, please."

She sighed. "I can feel when you're nearby."

My mouth dropped open in shock. She really could feel the bond.

"It's stupid, I know. I just get this sort of calming feeling whenever you're here, even if you're just hiding under the porch. I didn't understand that it was you until recently. You know, the first night you growled? I had been a little scared because Allen had shown up unexpectedly and was being a bit forward and pushy. But then you approached and this sort of calm ran through me and I knew I was going to be okay. I wasn't sure what the change was at the time, but then you growled. I started paying closer attention to my feelings and noticed a pattern. That peace always came when you arrived. I thought you were like my guardian angel or something."

"Mate," I said. "I'm your mate, but I had no idea you could feel it, too."

Katherine

Chapter 16

There was that word again. What did it mean?

I had so many questions rushing through my head. This was insane, yet James was here and, like always, I just knew everything would be okay as long as we were together. Maybe that made me psychotic. Maybe he should be the one running for the hills. But I couldn't control how he made me feel.

I wanted to ask, but I didn't dare. What did he mean when he called me his mate? In some countries that word meant nothing more than friend, yet it felt like so much more when he said it.

"What do you mean you didn't think I could feel it too?"

"Babe, you're human. There's some history of human shifter mates, true mates even, but it's not common. Humans aren't supposed to know about us. Do you understand? You can't tell anyone about me."

"Why?"

He looked at me like I was insane, and I could see his point.

"Oh, never mind. I get it. People who turn into wolves is supposed to be reserved for make-believe."

"Yeah, and that's where it needs to stay."

A thought suddenly occurred to me. "Are you telling me all of this now because of the baby? Will he be like you?"

"Or she," he said with a smirk.

"You know what I mean."

"It's possible. So regardless of whether you want me in your life or not, you need to know this stuff, for our child," he said as he reached out and lovingly stroked my belly with a sense of wonder in his eyes.

"*If* I want you in my life? Of course, I want you in my life. I need you, James. I've always needed you."

"It's your choice, babe."

"It doesn't feel like a choice. And what about you? Don't you get to choose?"

He shook his head. "No. My kind has this idea that God creates one male for every female. Only one, your true mate. It's a big world, so most shifters aren't lucky enough to find their one true mate."

"But you did? And that's me?"

He nodded.

"How long have you known?"

"Babe, I knew the second I met you that you were meant to be mine."

"But you left."

"You said you needed space."

"Space, not forever."

"I don't know much about human shifter relationships. I assumed you didn't feel the bond the same way I did."

"I was terrified by how powerful my feelings were for you. Everything was happening so fast, and I was trying to wrap my head around it. Then you were gone. You shredded my heart and took the pieces with you."

His face paled. "I didn't know," he whispered.

"Am I supposed to be incapable of feeling this connection you talk about just because I'm human?"

"I don't know. I just assumed."

This made me angrier than I knew possible.

"Well stop assuming and just ask me next time!" I screamed.

Emotions threatened to consume me again, but this time I refused to give into them.

"I'm sorry."

"Why were you in jail after we were together?" I demanded.

He visibly cringed.

"Tell me."

"It was too much, too powerful. I knew if I didn't stay away that I would claim you. I didn't think you felt the bond between us, Katherine. And there's more. I'm Sheriff of Collier. I took an oath to my job and my Alpha to protect the Pack, to put their needs ahead of my own. To tell you about my kind puts the entire Pack in jeopardy. I wanted to tell you so many times, but I couldn't. Don't you see?"

My jaw dropped open as I took in his words.

His Alpha.

His Pack.

There were more of these wolf shifters, a whole lot more.

"You're not part of a cult, you're all these, these shifters?"

He actually laughed. "There is no cult, though it's a lot easier to allow outsiders to believe that."

I nodded, finally putting some of the pieces together. It physically hurt knowing he didn't think he could trust me with all of this. But could he? If I hadn't seen him change, or shift, for myself, then I probably wouldn't have believed him anyway.

"Wait, is Lily a, um, shifter too?"

He hesitated, but then nodded.

"Katherine, this stays between you and me, are we clear? If anyone finds out that you know about this, it could put you in danger."

I scowled. "You said you'd never hurt me, that your kind wasn't a bunch of monsters."

"Many don't trust humans."

"I guess I can understand that. So basically, none of your kind can know that I know and none of my kind can know what you are?"

He nodded. "Yes. Though if I take you as my mate, the Pack will protect you, and our child."

"I thought I *am* your mate, your true mate, or whatever you called it?"

He looked frustrated. "There's more to it than that. There's a bond that's been created. Think of it as an invisible string connecting the two of us."

"Okay."

In some weird way that actually made sense to me.

"The more time we spend together, the stronger that string becomes, and the harder it is to break it."

"I'm following."

"It's why when we, uh, reconnected a few weeks ago, my wolf pressed for me to seal the bond with you."

"What does that mean? Seal the bond?"

"It's sort of like an unbreakable, binding marriage."

"No divorce?"

"Never."

"What if I die?"

He looked horrified by my question, but I didn't back down because I also wanted to know what happened if he died. Would this feeling, or connection that I couldn't deny between us also die?

He took in a sharp breath. "You're my true mate, Katherine, I may have questioned it and fought it in the past, but there's no denying it. You are mine. If you were to die, that would never change. I will not take another mate. Do I have the choice to do so? Yes, but I would not. And if say we grow old together and our bond…"

"This invisible string?"

He grinned and nodded. "Yes, that. If it seals, or think of it as becoming strong and thick enough to be solid and impenetrable, and you were to die, then I would peacefully follow you into death."

"You'd commit suicide?"

He chuckled. "No. But a fully sealed bond means that whatever happens to one of us, happens to the other. If you were to get cut and bleed, so would I."

"So if I were to die, then so would you?"

That was a lot to consider and far more of a commitment than I ever dreamed possible.

"It's not a bad thing. Honestly, it's like the highest achievement possible for a shifter to be that close and connected to someone."

Oh boy. Was that a good thing? Could I handle letting James in to that extent?

I waited a moment to let his words freak me out, but they didn't. In my heart, I was all in with him, and only him. There had never been another, not even close.

"Okay," I finally said.

"Okay?"

"I think I'm following. It's a lot to take in."

"I'm not asking you to make a decision right now, just keep an open mind, maybe?"

"I can do that," I assured him. "So, are all your friends, um, shifters?"

He hesitated.

"If I'm keeping an open mind, then so are you. You said that if we were to uh, seal this bond, then the Pack would protect me, but you also said they could never know. So that's a little confusing and I can't help but want to know more."

"This isn't easy for me to talk about, Katherine. Not even with you. I locked myself in a cell for weeks, apparently, to keep this from happening."

"What? That's why you were in jail? To avoid me?"

He nodded. "Yeah. My need to claim you, to tell you everything, was too strong. For me, you're like an addiction, and I attempted to detox from that after we were together. I'm not proud of it, but I did have my reasons for it."

"Obsession," I said.

"Huh?"

"You call it an addiction. I've already considered it more like an obsession, at least that's how it feels for me."

That wonder was back in his eyes as he reached out and touched my cheek.

"You really feel that? All of it?"

I nodded. "I feel so much I don't even know how to process it sometimes."

He leaned in so our foreheads touched and he seemed to sniff the air around us. I tried it too and was filled with the most mouth-watering delicious scent I'd ever smelled. I sighed in pleasure as it wrapped around me.

There was a knock on my front door and then it opened.

We both froze, and James let out a growl that made me all tingly inside.

"Are you expecting company?"

"No."

"Katherine? Are you here? One of your grocery bags got left in my van. I wanted to swing it by and check on you."

"Slugger, you can't just barge into someone else's home like this. Are you insane?"

They both stilled.

"What's that smell?" Lily asked. "Oh, gross. What is it? Katherine? Are you here? Is everything okay? Thomas, something's wrong."

"Nothing's wrong," I yelled. "And thanks for bringing that back. I'm fine."

I'd hoped that would be enough to get them to leave, but within seconds my door burst open, making James and I jump.

He growled menacingly as I cowered behind him.

Thomas sniffed the air and crinkled his nose.

"Really? That was necessary?"

I sniffed the air again, only smelling that sweet aroma I loved so much.

"Shut up," James said.

"So, what's going on here?" Lily asked. "Aren't you supposed to be in rehab?"

He growled at her.

"Careful, James," Thomas warned, and there suddenly was this weird static electricity filling the air. It made my skin tingle in an unpleasant way.

"What was that? Did you feel that? And why are you growling at them? I thought they were your friends."

"They are," he insisted.

"You felt that?" Lily asked.

Thomas shot her a look of warning, but Lily just studied me closely.

I leaned over and whispered as softly as I could in James's ear.

"Are they shifters too?"

Thomas looked shocked. "You told her? You actually told her?"

"About damn time, if you ask me," Lily insisted.

My eyes widened in surprise.

"H-how did you hear that? There's no way you heard me."

"Super hearing," Lily said as she pointed to her ears.

"Oh," I squeaked.

"Are we going to have a problem here, Thomas?" James asked.

"How much did you tell her?"

"Enough."

"Wait, there's more?" I asked.

"Oh, girl, so much more."

"Lily!" the two men warned.

"Well the cat's out of the bag now, or wolf, or whatever. You are not keeping me in the dark anymore."

"Ladies' night soon. Let's plan it. We'll fill you in on all the things," Lily practically squealed.

It was then that I remembered James's warning and shook my head.

"No, I can't. I'm not supposed to know about any of this. You aren't supposed to know I know."

"Who told you that?" she demanded as I cut my eyes towards James.

Lily smacked him.

"Ow."

"Why would you tell her that? She's pregnant with your child, you idiot. She needs to know these things and she needs the support of the Pack."

"We haven't gotten that far yet," he muttered.

"He hasn't, uh, claimed me or anything," I said, hoping I got the words right.

"Hold up," Thomas barked. "She's pregnant? When did this happen?"

"Keep up. And seriously? I'm pretty sure we walked into the aftermath of that conception, remember?"

My jaw went slack and my cheeks burned as I hid my face in James's back.

"Really? She's pregnant?" he asked James.

Slowly he nodded. "Yes, she's pregnant and I sort of wolfed out over it."

"Reverse wolfed out? Human-ed out?" I asked trying to get the right words.

Lily laughed. "What does that even mean?"

"I don't know. He was a wolf and then he wasn't. So what do you call that? Wolfed out sounds like he just suddenly changed into a wolf."

146

"Stalking her again?"

James just grinned and shrugged. "You're the one who demanded they let me out. You had to know I'd end up here. I tried to tell you I wasn't ready."

"But this is good."

"Is it?" I asked. "Because right now I sort of feel like I'm stuck in a dream and can't wake up, but know none of its real."

"Oh, it's real," Lily assured me. "Take some time to absorb it, but now that you're in the know, I've got your back. We're going to be great friends."

"Are you trying to scare her away, slugger?" Thomas teased as she stuck her tongue out at him. "Don't go making promises you don't intend to keep."

Lily blushed then seemed to instantly recover. "Who said I didn't intend to keep it?"

Thomas grinned like a fool and the love between them was evident.

"Are you two fully bonded?" I blurted out.

Thomas seemed intrigued by my question, but Lily just shrugged it off.

"Bonded yes, fully, not yet, but hopefully someday."

"Is there a way to know for sure then?" I asked, wanting to know everything I could about this bonding stuff.

"Well, yeah…"

"Lily, some things are best left for her mate to explain," Thomas warned, shaking his head.

"Whatever. Are you planning on accepting him as your mate then?"

I didn't understand what she meant.

"I thought he was my mate."

"I was trying to explain some things when you two barged in. It's been a lot for one night," James insisted, and while I wanted to know everything right now, I also was sort of feeling overwhelmed by everything I had learned, so I couldn't disagree with him.

"We should probably leave them be. Are you staying here tonight?" Thomas asked James.

"I don't know. Just give us some space, okay?"

"Are we going to be in some sort of trouble?" I asked. "I mean you said your kind shouldn't know that I know, and now they know. I don't want to get any of you in trouble. Is there some sort of hierarchy or something? Alpha, you mentioned an Alpha, that's like the leader, right? Like in a wolf Pack? Oh no, did I just call you all animals? Is that wrong? Am I screwing it all up?"

Lily walked over and gave me a hug.

"You're doing great, sweetie. And yes, there is a Pack hierarchy, but you don't need to worry about that. I have it on good authority that his Alpha will be very understanding of your situation, and if not, I'll punch him in the balls, because I like you and promise nothing bad will happen to you within Collier Pack."

"What?"

Thomas laughed. "Subtle."

I looked up at Thomas with understanding.

"You're the Alpha?"

"I am, but I'm also his best friend and very much pro true mates. I was lucky enough to find my own and would never deny any of my wolves that, human or not. I'll admit, I was a little skeptical when he first told me. You guys have known each other a long time to have an unresolved bond like that."

"Is that a bad thing?"

"It can be," he said as a haunted look crossed his face. "But I can feel your bond. It's surprisingly strong and healthy. You aren't freaking out and fighting this, are you?"

I looked from him back to James.

"Should I be?"

"No!" all three of them said before laughing.

"That's always your choice, of course," Lily added. "But Thomas and I are rooting for you and trust me, fighting it only hurts more."

"You fought yours?"

Thomas snorted. "That's a story for another day. I need to get this one home and in bed. Mom stayed over with the girls for us, but only until we get back. Trust me, mornings with our pups can be exhausting. I guess you'll see soon enough."

As they left, I placed my hand on my stomach and turned my worried eyes to James.

"Pups?"

James
Chapter 17

We stayed up late talking as I tried to clear up some things Thomas and Lily had said and things Katherine had inferred from what she'd learned.

Her biggest concern had been giving birth to an actual puppy. When I explained that wasn't going to happen and how shifters didn't get their animal spirit until they were considered adults, she started to relax.

Talking to Katherine about all of this was surprisingly much easier than I expected.

"What do you have going on today?" I asked her, noting we were well into a new day.

"Nothing," she sighed. "You?"

"I have to swing into the office tomorrow to go over a few things. Would you, um, like to join me?"

"Really?" she asked perking up. "Like into Collier County?"

"We call it Collier Pack."

"Right. At least now I understand why you guys are so rude to outsiders."

"We don't mean to be. Honestly, many shifters are just scared of humans. I mean, you're taking all of this remarkably well. Most wouldn't."

"Well, I'm also a bit relieved that there's a reason behind the way I feel about you and I'm not just obsessively certifiable."

I laughed. "Well, I didn't say that."

She nudged me with her arm and then yawned.

"What time is it?"

"Four in the morning. Tired?"

"Exhausted."

"Try to get some sleep."

"Are you, um, staying?"

"Do you want me to?"

"Yes," she said, a little too forcefully. It made me smile.

"Then I'm not going anywhere."

"Good. Because if you aren't here in the morning, I'm going to consider myself officially crazy and check myself into rehab."

I laughed. "Tried that, it doesn't help."

"Not even a little?"

"I'm here, aren't I?"

"Just can't stay away?"

"Something like that."

"Good."

She rolled over and rested her head on my chest as she yawned once more.

"Because I don't intend on ever letting you go again," she said in a sleepy voice as she drifted off to sleep.

*****

I would never tire of waking up with Katherine in my arms. For a moment I thought just maybe I'd dreamt it all, but I hadn't. She was here and this was real.

"Mine," I whispered as I kissed the top of her head.

"Fine, but I'm starving," she murmured in a sleepy voice.

"Kate's for breakfast? My treat?"

"But that's in Collier County, er, Pack."

151

"It is."

"So we don't need to hide there now?"

I shrugged. "It would probably be for the best, but Thomas and Lily already know and gave their blessings. The others won't dare say anything about it."

"But I'll still be an outsider?"

"It's possible. Honestly, I don't know. We have a few half-breeds in the Pack but no actual humans that I'm aware of."

"Half-breeds?"

I cringed. "One of their parents is human."

"No," she said. "We are *not* calling our kid, or our pup, or whatever, a half-breed."

I grinned. "Yes ma'am. I shall never use that term again."

"Do you know how damaging that can be psychologically to a child?"

"No, but I'm sure you're going to educate me on it. But for now, get dressed and let's eat. I'm starving."

There was a familiarity about how we moved around the bedroom and bathroom as we got ready for the day. It was like no time had passed at all between us.

I didn't have my car with me since I'd run over in my fur, so I drove hers to Kate's Diner.

It was a busy morning and the place was packed, but as we walked in hand-in-hand, everyone stopped and stared.

Katherine shot me a concerned look.

"Just ignore them," I whispered, even knowing they would all hear me. And then I did the one thing that every wolf in the place recognized. I scented my mate.

Within minutes several people were scrambling to leave and others gawked with open curiosity as they held their noses and ate.

"Oh look, a table," I said happily.

"You did that thing again, didn't you?"

"I don't know what you're talking about," I said innocently.

"Yes you do, because this whole place smells like you now."

"Is that a good thing?"

"The best," she said. "But I don't think the other people here would agree. Why is that?"

"I'll explain later," I said with a wink.

Kate came over personally to take our order.

"Was that really necessary?" she asked.

"Yes," I assured her.

"You ran off half of my morning customers."

"Then they shouldn't have been making my mate uncomfortable. Kate, this is Katherine, Katherine, Kate."

"So you're doing this? Finally?"

I frowned. "Wyatt already told you?"

"Everything."

"Wyatt? That's one of your Six Pack brothers, right?"

Kate softened and smiled down at her.

"The best of them all."

Katherine considered that and shook her head.

"No, pretty sure, I got that one."

"Nice. You might just make the cut around here with that kind of attitude. What are you having?"

We gave her our orders and she went back to the kitchen to get them started. I reached down and started the stopwatch feature on my phone.

"What are you doing?"

"Seeing how long they take to get here."

"Who?"

"The guys. There's zero chance that Kate didn't rush back there and call Wyatt. Like a bunch of freaking gossips, he'll put calls out alerting the others."

"You think they'll just show up here?"

"I can guarantee it."

Kate swung by with coffee refills for the both of us just as Thomas and Lily arrived.

"That's one," I whispered.

Lily frowned and snagged the coffee cup away from Katherine just as Wyatt, Clay, Winnie, Austin, and Emmett all rushed in.

"Hey," Katherine protested.

"You can't have coffee. It's bad for the baby," Lily blurted out, causing my friends to stop in their tracks and the rest of the diner to go silent once more. Then she grabbed my cup as well. "Be more supportive here. If she can't have it, neither can you."

"Sorry, man. I can't even remember the last time I was allowed a cup," Thomas said.

"We had coffee just the other week."

Lily scowled at him. "You did what?"

"You're an ass," Thomas muttered down to me. "Decaf, slugger. It was decaf."

"Sure it was," I murmured under my breath.

"You'll pay for this," Thomas warned me.

"She took my coffee. I'm pretty sure I'm already paying for it."

"You're pregnant?" Emmett blurted out as all eyes and ears turned towards us.

Katherine didn't back down even a second. She raised her chin with conviction and looked him square in the eyes.

"Yes, I am."

I was going to have to warn her about that. Making direct eye contact with a wolf and holding the stare like that was a direct challenge. Thankfully, Emmett just laughed.

"Well ain't that some shit. Do we know who the daddy is?"

"Don't be an ass," I told him as he laughed harder and an extra table was added on the end of ours to make room for everyone.

Lily and Winnie scooted in on Katherine's side in this weird sort of protective stance leaving no doubt that they had her back.

"Thank you," I mouthed to Lily, but knowing how fiercely protective she was of all of us, I knew I didn't have to.

Katherine was mine, and that made her Pack. Not just that, it made her family, Six Pack family.

No doubt the news would travel quickly throughout the Pack, but with Thomas's acceptance I knew no one would dare say a word about it.

Soon the food was plentiful and everyone's spirits were high. Several people stopped by just to be a part of what would no doubt go down as the biggest shocking news of the year, and others came by just to congratulate me.

Katherine remained relaxed and comfortable, which kept my wolf calm.

Peyton came out of the kitchen to check out the commotion for herself. I was quick to introduce her to my mate. She was one of Thomas's sisters and a good ally for Katherine. If anyone understood the challenges of raising a half-human child in this Pack, it was Peyton. Her mate, his three brothers, and her oldest daughter were all half-breeds, er, half-human. They seemed to work through it just fine, but then none of them were actually human themselves.

"Peyton, this is Katherine."

"Hi," Peyton said.

"Oh, good call," Lily told me. "Pey, you and Katherine need to get together soon. You should be friends for sure."

I rolled my eyes.

"Subtle, Lil."

"We've met," Katherine surprised me by saying. "Under, not so pleasant circumstances."

I wracked my brain to think of when that would have happened and then remembered.

"Oh shit. You were on the case regarding custody of Eve. I forgot all about that."

"It's okay. You were just doing your job," Peyton said graciously.

"Whatever. Water under the bridge now. Oh, are you girls thinking what I'm thinking?" Lily squealed.

"Doubtful," Winnie admitted.

"Ladies' night!"

"Absolutely not," I protested shooting my mate a warning look. I couldn't fathom the amount of trouble this group could manage, though I'd certainly heard enough of the rumors.

"We're long overdue," Lily said completely ignoring me.

"I'm in," Katherine stubbornly said, despite my warning.

"Yes!" Lily cheered. "I'll get right on it." She tossed a wadded-up napkin at me. "Relax, it's not like we can drink or anything."

I snorted and shook my head.

"We can have it at my house," Peyton offered. "We're long overdue for this. Sounds like fun."

"Okay, I'll make some calls. How about tomorrow night?"

I groaned. "Seriously?"

"Absolutely!"

The guys started to heckle me, but when Wyatt and Clay joined in, I was quick to point out that their mates should be there too. That shut them both up pretty quickly.

Overall, I was pleased with how welcoming my friends were being. Maybe, just maybe, everything would work out okay after all.

After breakfast I drove us over to the jailhouse. It was true that I had a few things to do, okay, I had a lot of things to do after all the time I'd taken off.

I was surprised to find Julian there when we arrived.

"Hey Sheriff."

"Julian, is everything okay?"

"Sure," he said nodding towards the cells.

"Harlan, what are you doing back here?"

"Had to get away from that woman. She's crazy, tried to throw out my beer," he said slurring his words. "Needed a quiet place for the night."

"Harlan," Katherine whispered. "Wait, he's naked. He was the naked guy in here before, too, wasn't he? Oh, was he also the staggering wolf in the road that you ran off?"

I sighed and rolled my eyes, but nodded. Did she have to be so observant?

"Who's this?" Harlan asked.

I scowled. I hadn't meant to integrate her into the Pack so quickly, but after the scene at Kate's, I knew it was too late for that.

"This is Katherine, my mate."

Julian grinned.

"You already knew?"

He shrugged. "Ryder's sister's best friend was in the diner when you came in and caused quite the ruckus. Did you really have to scent the whole place? Heard it was some kind of disgusting."

"I like how you smell," Katherine assured me.

I grinned. "You're supposed to."

I pulled her into my arms and dropped a quick kiss on her lips, claiming her in a different way.

"As his mate, it's supposed to smell like the best scent ever to you. But to everyone else in unfortunate proximity, it's a warning scent that makes a grown man gag. So gross," Julian explained.

I shrugged unapologetically.

"I made the point that needed to be made."

"Oh yeah, what's that?"

"That you're mine," I said, kissing her again.

"Aw, that is so sweet. Almost makes me want to run home to my mate… almost," Harlan said with a cackle.

I laughed and reached for her hand.

"Come on, I won't be long."

Inside my office I shut the door and then turned on the dampener.

"What's that?"

"It's called a dampener. Wolves have really great hearing, and this is the only way I can have any privacy."

She bit her lip. "So they can't hear or see anything going on in here?"

"Nope. We're completely alone."

"Can I, um, ask you something?"

"Anything," I said, looking up as she stepped between me and my desk.

"Anything?"

"I don't want any more secrets between us, Katherine. Ask me anything."

"That smell that everyone complains about?"

"Yeah?"

"Is it normal for it to make me super horny? I mean, it's like the ultimate aphrodisiac."

She wrapped her arms around me and kissed me hard.

With everything that had happened, I'd purposefully tried not to touch her, at least not in a way that escalated things physically, but there was no way in hell I was going to stop this.

I couldn't have stopped myself if I wanted to as I quickly stripped her out of her clothes and laid her bare across my desk before devouring her. She was the best thing I'd ever tasted, and I couldn't get enough as her hands fisted in my hair, keeping me close as I made her come on my tongue.

As soon as she climaxed, I jumped up, undid my pants and pushed them to the floor. I dragged her off the desk and turned her around. Placing her hands on top of the desk, I took her harder than I meant to as I claimed her with each thrust, both overpowering and cradling her in a warring battle of need and love.

I had never been so primal with her. There was nothing gentle about it this time as I struggled against the urge to mark her as mine. It wasn't time yet. She needed to understand what she was getting herself into. So instead, I marked her with my hands as I gripped her hips harder than I should have and my mouth as I sucked on the spot I hoped to someday seal my bond with her, satisfied with at least a temporary mark on her otherwise flawless skin.

My rhythm faltered as my balls started to tighten sooner than I'd have liked. I growled in frustration but as she started to tighten around me, alerting me to her climax too, I let go, lifting my head and howling through my release as she shattered in my arms.

Panting and sweaty with my legs shaking, I sat back down in the chair, pulling her with me still deep inside of her. I wasn't ready to let her go.

Our ragged breaths mingled as her lips found mine and she smiled against them, sending a shiver down my spine.

"I guess it makes you a little crazy, too, huh?"

I barked out a laugh from her unexpected words.

"I didn't mean to get so carried away. I didn't hurt you, did I?"

She jumped up and I immediately missed our physical connection, but then she turned around and straddled me. Her hands ran through my hair as she studied my face.

"Today's been a lot, but I'm not some fragile doll, James. That was amazing and I think we both needed it."

I smiled against her lips as I kissed her once more.

Katherine
Chapter 18

Sex with James had always been good, but now, it was out of this world great. I had to force myself not to think about the whole wolf thing or it freaked me out a little. I still had so many questions and if he actually wolfed out during *that,* I would... well, I don't know what I'd do, but that's a hard no for me. Though his growling and howling certainly don't bother me any, but that's where I draw the line.

"You don't have to go tonight. You could just stay home with me," he said with a grin.

"We've already been through this, James. We've spent nearly every second of the last forty-eight hours together. If you want me to fit into your world, then I need to do this."

"But they're all insane. If you have questions or anything, you can just ask me."

"Have you ever, you know, turned into a wolf while having sex?" I blurted out.

His jaw dropped and then he fully belly laughed.

"Great. See, this is why I do need other women to talk to."

"Babe, I'm not laughing at you. It just took me by surprise. I would never do that to you."

"But is it... you know... like a thing?"

He chuckled again, and I wasn't sure if he was taking me serious or not.

"No, at least not that I'm aware of. I suppose like any other fetish maybe someone somewhere, but no one I know would do that."

"You're sure?"

"I'm sure, Katherine. There are shifters who do it in their fur, but both are in their fur and it is usually only for procreation to repopulate our species."

"You can do that?"

He nodded seriously this time.

"We were designed for that, and with the extinction of certain animals it could be necessary. See when we procreate in our fur, we produce animals. They aren't human, they don't have a human spirit at all, they're just animals. It's not something we take lightly, and it weighs heavily on the shifters. The female can't even shift out of her fur when that happens, and likewise, in human form. Like right now Lily's pregnant, she can't shift into her fur until the baby is born. It's when our females are most vulnerable."

I considered that for a moment and then frowned.

"Does that mean I'm always vulnerable then?"

"To an extent, but you have full Pack protection. Thomas is already seeing to it."

"Why do I need protection?"

He sighed and ran a hand over his weeks' old beard.

"Not everyone will understand us or even recognize our bond."

"What? Why not? Wait, because I'm just a human?"

He nodded sadly. "Yeah. They're ignorant and don't understand."

"They don't think it's possible for a human like me to actually bond with someone like you," I guessed.

He nodded again. "Like I said, they're ignorant."

"James, where will that leave our child?"

"Partially torn between two worlds. But we will love her and raise her to be strong."

"Or him," I corrected.

He rolled his eyes. "Or him."

"You think we're having a girl, don't you?"

He grinned. "Just a hunch."

"I'm not even sure this kid has those parts yet. It's way too early for a hunch, James."

He just laughed and shrugged.

"You want a daughter?"

"I want a healthy pup."

I cringed. That word creeped me out. A pup? I was going to give birth to a dog?

"A baby, Katherine. It's just another term for a baby. Don't read too much into it."

"I still can't even believe it. I mean, it happened so fast that a part of me feels like it was just a dream, or I imagined it or something."

"What? Me shifting from a wolf to me right in front of you?"

"Yes!"

"Do you want to see it again?"

"You'd do that?"

"The wolf's kind of out of the bag for us already."

"So how does it work then?"

He shrugged. "I really don't know how to explain that to you."

"Does it hurt?"

"No."

"Not even a little?"

"No. We don't start to shift until we reach maturity, most often that's anywhere from eighteen to twenty-two. It's not uncommon for someone as young as sixteen though, and there are documented cases as young as at least twelve."

"And it doesn't hurt at all?"

"No."

"But how is that possible?"

"I honestly don't know; it's just how it is. Would you like to see it?"

"Yes."

He stood up and started taking his clothes off.

I glared at him. "Would you keep your clothes on. You aren't going to persuade me not to go tonight."

James laughed. "That's not what I'm doing, but I do like where your mind is."

"Then why are you stripping for me?"

"You said you wanted to see me shift."

"And you have to be naked for it?"

"No, but it sure beats buying new clothes all the time."

"What?"

"Katherine, my clothes aren't made of magic or anything. If I shift in them, they end up a shredded pile on the floor."

"Oh. Really? Like the Hulk or something?"

"Exactly like the Hulk."

"Oh, is that why Harlan was naked in jail again?"

He snorted. "Yes."

"Okay, I guess that makes sense."

"Ready?"

"I'm not sure I'll ever fully be ready for this," I confessed.

He gave me a sad look for only a second before he morphed, or shifted, or whatever he called it into a wolf, a freaking wolf!

"Wow!"

He walked up to me as he'd done before and watched me curiously, probably to see if I was going to freak out.

"I'm okay," I assured him. "It's just so surreal. Can I, um, pet you?"

I felt like an idiot talking to this animal before me, but when he nodded his big head, the reality hit me hard that this was still James, my James.

"It's really you in there, isn't it?"

He nodded his head once more.

"And you can understand everything I'm saying."

The wolf's head moved up and down again.

I reached out hesitantly with my hand, but he closed the gap and rubbed against it. Soon he was rubbing up against my legs and trying to climb into my lap. I should have been terrified, but he was wagging his tail and in some weird way I could feel his happiness.

Then, he licked my cheek.

"Gross. Cut it out. That tongue only gets near me in human form. You got that, mister?"

He started chuffing and I could have sworn it was James laughing at me, but he stepped back and seemed to respect the boundaries, though not before he rubbed up against my legs again.

"Why do you keep doing that?"

James shifted back, standing gloriously naked before me.

"Because my wolf wants to put our scent all over you. It's another, less *intrusive*, way of warning off unmated males in the area."

"Without gagging them all?"

"Exactly."

A knock on the door told me my time was up... for now.

"That's probably Lily. She insisted on picking me up, like I don't know where the Smith house is already."

He smiled and grabbed a pair of sweatpants to throw on. I was already gathering that nudity really wasn't a big deal amongst shifters, but I was grateful for it. I didn't like the idea of every woman seeing my man like that.

"She's a good friend to have around here, Katherine."

"Pack Mother, highest ranking female," I repeated from an earlier lesson on Pack hierarchy.

"Well that, and because Thomas really is my best friend and she's his mate."

I nodded. He didn't need to worry though. Lily could be overbearing and determined at times, but it was really hard not to like her. She just had that sort of personality that could make everyone feel like they were someone special.

I gave James a quick kiss and answered the door.

"Hi Lily."

She responded by hugging me. That was something else I was learning without being told. These wolves seemed to be quite the touchy-feely bunch, which was hysterical given their penchant for snubbing outsiders. With each touch or hug I felt like maybe I really could do this. Just maybe, I wouldn't always be "the human" or an outsider looking in.

"Ready?"

"Lily, you better behave and watch out for my woman tonight."

She just laughed as she linked her arm through mine.

"Don't worry so much. Us preggers are gonna stick together."

Ack! Preggers? I was pregnant. That was the other shocking news I hadn't fully come to terms with yet. Between that and all this shifter stuff, I truly felt like I was living in a dream, or an alternate reality at the very least.

Lily dragged me from the house and into her car.

"How many people are going to be there tonight?"

"Oh, not many. You don't need to worry. It's just Peyton, then us plus Kate, and Winnie, of course because the four of us now make up the Six Pack ladies. Two more to go! Then Thomas's other sisters Ruby and Clara, and Sydney, she's my best friend and Thomas's ex-lover. That's it for tonight. I didn't want to overwhelm you or anything."

"That's small?"

I tended to be more of a loner, I supposed. Raised as an only child, I often struggled with fitting in with my peers. I had always gotten along with adults better, or children. I adored children which was why I chose the field I was in. Helping kids meant the world to me, I really didn't need much more than that to feel satisfied with my life, or so I thought.

Don't get me wrong, I did have friends, just not close ones. There wasn't even anyone I could think of besides my parents that I really needed to call and explain my whole baby news to.

This ladies' night with a bunch of women was not something I'd ever done before, and I had no idea what to expect.

"Are all these women like you and James?"

She looked confused for a moment and then laughed.

"You mean are they all shifters?"

"Yup, that's what I meant."

"Of course. Everyone in Collier is."

I gulped hard. "Everyone?"

I supposed I knew that. I mean it made sense. They were a Pack, and a Pack meant more than one, but all of them?

"That's so many," I blurted out.

She grinned and nodded. "We're one of the larger packs, but not the largest."

"Wait, there's more of you out there?"

"Oh honey, there's a lot more of us than you'd think. We just live normal human lives under the radar so as not to showcase our, uh, differences."

"That's one way to put it," I mumbled.

"There aren't just wolf shifters either, did James explain that?"

"What? No. What does that mean? There're more than werewolves out there, or sorry, wolf shifters?"

"A lot more."

She pulled up to the pretty white house with the large wrap around porch where Peyton and her husband, Oliver, live. Oliver had a daughter, Eve, who's biological mother had filed charges against them for custody of the child. It had been an awkward mess in the end. The woman had lied and tried to manipulate me, believing that

CPS always sides with the mother. She was wrong. My job is to only ever side with the best interests of the child.

There had been no doubt in my mind that the little girl was exactly where she needed to be, but they had taken steps further to secure parental rights for not just Oliver, but via adoption post abandonment, for Peyton, too.

It was a little underhanded how they'd stripped the bio mom's rights, but at the same time, she had run off and left her baby, she had lied to the courts on those circumstances, and she had tried to use me for her own personal gain.

In the end everything had worked out in the best interest of the child without me really having to do anything. That was a good thing too, because James had reappeared out of the blue for the case, and I had been in no condition to actually do my job after not having seen him in a long time.

The way that man affected my emotions was insane, but I supposed it was just this bond thing the entire time.

"Okay, get out of your head, and into this house. We are happy to answer any questions, but do know, you'll be interrogated plenty yourself," Lily warned with an evil grin on her face.

The aroma of mouth-watering food hit me before we even reached the porch.

"What is that?"

Lily grinned. "Peyton. That girl is a master chef, for real, certified and all, and makes the most amazing foods. Why do you think no one ever complains when she wants to host these things?"

Her laughter was still ringing through the air as she opened the door without knocking and let herself in.

"Grab some food, we're back here," Peyton yelled from somewhere in the house.

Lily seemed to know what she meant though. We grabbed plates and piled on the amazing foods she'd set out before walking down the hall and into what looked like a giant playroom, living room combination.

Three little girls sat on the floor playing with a pile of toys.

Lily frowned. "No one told me to bring the girls."

"Sorry, Brady volunteered, but we had a last-minute emergency at the dairy and I sure as hell wasn't missing this. He'll be along shortly to take them off our hands," a redhead explained.

"Katherine, this is Ruby and that's Clara," she said pointing to a brunette sitting on the couch who gave me a little wave.

I waved back. "Hi."

"Make yourself comfortable, Katherine. Do you know everyone else here already?" Peyton asked as I took a seat on the couch between Kate and Winnie.

I looked around and stopped on the one I didn't know.

"Oh, this is Sydney," Lily piped in.

I concentrated on the name and then nodded. "Thomas's ex-lover."

The woman scowled. "Lily!"

"What? It's true!"

"That was a long time ago, before Lily came to town."

"Everyone thought she and Thomas would mate. They were on-again off-again since they hit puberty right up until the day little Lily Westin rolled into town," Ruby explained.

"Then what happened?" I asked, not fully understanding.

"Oh, they're true mates," Clara said. "Rocked our baby brother's world, but not in the good kind of way, at least not at first."

The girls hooted with laughter that I didn't really understand.

"Guys, you have to explain it," Peyton told them. "See, it's a long crazy story, but our sister Maddie went missing as a teen."

"MC and I are super close, more like sisters than best friends," Lily chimed in.

"Anyway," Peyton continued. "Thomas didn't really handle her disappearance well and he'd ghost out on anything that reminded him of her."

"Including the annual vigil the Pack held, and Lily took that to mean he was a douchebag," Ruby added.

"There were other reasons," Lily insisted. "But whatever. The mating bond makes you crazy and I probably could have handled it better."

The room erupted in laughter once more and I knew there was a lot more to the story than what they were sharing. Still, it was nice to know that mating for her had been unnerving too.

"Are all of you mated?" I asked, hoping I didn't screw up their terminology too badly.

"Yes," Peyton said.

"And was it crazy for all of you, too?"

This just caused more laughter that I didn't understand.

"Wyatt and I didn't fight our bond, but we did wait a long time to seal it which caused its own issues. We were just so young at the time," Kate explained.

"Yeah, Clay and I didn't really fight ours either," Winnie said.

"What are you talking about? I caught you climbing out of his bedroom window to get away," Lily reminded her, causing Winnie to blush.

"Fine, maybe I didn't handle it quite as well as I like to think."

"Well, I certainly didn't fight it," Ruby said.

"No, you sealed your bond before you even knew Bran's name," Clara said.

"As if you were much better," Peyton challenged.

Clara shrugged. "I didn't exactly fight it, he did. That's not my fault."

"How about you, Peyton?"

"Oh, I knew exactly what I wanted the second I met Oliver."

"Yeah, and she orchestrated the entire thing while he swore he'd never claim her," Lily informed me.

Peyton shrugged. "Sometimes you just have to fight for your family."

"But I thought wolves wanted to find, or claim, or whatever, their mate?" So much of this was still confusing to me.

"Oh, for sure. It's in our nature," Sydney explained. "But emotions are real and make you sometimes do crazy things. We are still human too and crave the control of free will."

I frowned. "And you don't have free will?"

She shrugged. "I mean there is one person out there that you're destined to be with. When you meet him, everything inside you is designed to be with him, only him. Do we have a choice in that?" she shrugged. "They tell us we do, but no one really understands how to break that bond, so you're constantly driven back to him."

I thought back through my relationship with James. Since the moment we met, I really did know I was destined to be with him. He was my perfect match right down to our stubborn natures that had ultimately driven us apart. Yet every time our paths crossed the chemistry between us was tangible. That hasn't changed, even knowing there was some divine power out there orchestrating it all. It didn't change how I felt about him.

"Don't," Kate warned.

"Don't what?" I asked.

"Overthink it. I can practically hear the gears turning in your brain. Yes, if we stop to think about it, we all have those wonders and fears. Is this my choice? Do I have any control over this situation? But in the end, does it even matter? Wyatt makes me happier than any other person on this planet, hands down. He's my teddy bear, my comfort zone, my everything. So why do I even care how it happened? I'm just really grateful it did."

The others all nodded in agreement.

"Was I that transparent?"

"Yes," Sydney assured me. "And I didn't mean to freak you out."

"Actually, you didn't. It makes more sense than it probably should."

"So we're all dying to know what it's like for you, as a human," Ruby pressed.

"Ruby," Lily warned.

"Oh please, like you're not all thinking it."

"I don't know what you mean? Why would it be any different for me?"

She shrugged. "So much of the mating process is integrated into our wolves that we really don't know."

I frowned. "Your wolves?"

"Yeah, from the second we meet our mates, our wolves start alerting us. 'Mine', 'mate' stuff like that in our heads over and over to the point of annoying."

"James says those things all the time."

"Well yeah. His wolf is probably losing his shit not being able to reach yours."

I had never considered something like that.

"Ruby!" Lily warned again.

"Is that something that happens?" I asked, ignoring Ruby's warnings.

"It does for us, but we honestly don't know how it works for you," Lily admitted. "Like do you feel… I don't even know how to ask this because I can't say the bond and expect you to know what that feels like."

"Obsessed," I admitted. "It's hard to control sometimes. When we were originally together it was so intense that it terrified me. He wanted to settle down and get married."

"Married?" Winnie asked. "We don't do the whole marriage thing."

"You don't?"

"No. Bonding is so much stronger than that. What's the point?"

"Oh," I said.

"If James asked you to marry him, then he damn well knew what he was doing and the importance of that for you," Ruby argued.

The others nodded in agreement.

"So, what happened then?" Clara asked.

"We were young, too young, or so I thought. I didn't think this feeling would last forever."

Kate laughed. "Total human thing to say."

I rolled my eyes but smiled. "How was I supposed to know people like you existed outside of movies and books?"

"So he asked and you said no?" Clara asked.

"Did he get down on one knee and everything?" Sydney added.

"Not exactly, and yes, ring and all. I didn't say no. I just kind of freaked out and told him I thought we should slow things down some."

"Damn girl, you have no idea how much that must have angered his wolf," Ruby said shaking her head.

"I didn't know," I said quietly.

"Well, if he asks again, just say yes," Peyton advised.

"But why would he? You guys just said marriage doesn't mean anything."

She shrugged. "Sometimes it does. I mean Oliver and I are bonded but also legally married. We did it for Eve when custody was threatened."

"Oh, right."

As if she knew we were talking about her, the little girl got up and ran over to climb in her mother's lap. Just then a man walked in. Man, he was hot. Still, I felt nothing more than an appreciation of his good looks. As I thought back, it's been that way ever since I first met James.

"Speak of the devil himself," Ruby teased. "Katherine, this is Brady. Brady, Katherine. She's human. We were just explaining the whole half-breed thing to her."

Brady's jaw dropped and his brow furrowed.

"Why?" he blurted out. "Since when do we tell humans anything? You can't trust them. They'll just turn on you and call you a monster."

"She's James's mate," Lily warned.

"Shit. I heard he took a mate, but she's really human? And she knows about us?" He looked me over with a mix of shock and disgust on his face. "And you didn't run away screaming with nightmares?"

I snorted. "I mean, the night's still early."

Winnie giggled.

"Brady, she's handling everything great."

"Whatever. It's nice to meet you, I guess. I'll take the girls upstairs and give you guys some space."

He bent down and let Eve jump on his back with a squeal before he walked over and swooped up two more girls, one in each arm and left.

"Don't mind him. He has his reasons for that," Peyton said softly.

I nodded, but his harsh tone was a little unnerving.

"Your daughter, is her, you know, bio mom, also a wolf?" I asked.

"No. Eve is half human just like your kids will be someday. Oliver and all three of his brothers are too."

"Wait, isn't Brady one of Oliver's brothers?" I blurted out.

"Yes. His mother didn't handle it well and left them with an abusive alcoholic father," Peyton explained. "I won't say it'll always be easy and that every shifter you meet will be open minded, but most of us have nothing against humans. Like I said, he has his reasons."

"But he's a half-breed as you call them, which I hate that name, by the way."

"Not my favorite either. I know it's something I'll have to protect my daughter from, especially as she gets older."

"Me too," I said softly. "I don't mean to ask so many questions and please stop me if I'm being rude."

"No, it's fine, and you're doing great. It's good for them to see that not all humans are like their mother, you know?"

I nodded, understanding exactly what she meant.

"Okay, so if Eve's bio parents are human and a half human shifter, does that make her a quarter wolf then?" I wondered aloud, trying to put all the pieces together.

"No, we still consider it half since her father has his wolf. If Oliver had never gotten his wolf spirit, then I believe that would make her a quarter shifter, in which case there would still be a small chance that she could still get a wolf spirit."

"That can happen even if neither of her parents had one?"

"Yup. If there's shifter blood in your family tree, then it's always a possibility."

"It's rare though," Lily said. "But could happen where even several generations have gone dormant and then, surprise! We have a new shifter. Okay, I've never actually known anyone that happened to, but my mother says it's possible."

"Genetics would agree," Clara insisted. "It's like the mysterious ginger gene in my opinion, where everything has to align perfectly for that to happen, but totally possible."

"I can't even imagine," Winnie said with a shiver. "To just discover something like that on your own? That would be so scary."

"My brother's mate, Kelsey, was orphaned as a kid. She suffered a traumatic event and shifted alone without any knowledge of what she was. She honestly thought she was a monster, a werewolf. She didn't know people like us existed, yet she moved into wolf pack territory and took a job completely oblivious to it all."

"I bet that went over well. You guys aren't exactly open to outsiders."

"Yeah, no one understood why she wasn't run out of town. We all knew she was wolf, but it took a few years before we found out that she had no clue about us."

"Years? How is that even possible?"

"Well, my big brother is Alpha of Westin Pack and her true mate. He was protecting her all along. Boy did she drive him insane."

"It's not quite the same, but it happened to Emmy Kenston, too," Sydney said.

"Emmy Kenston, like Alicia Kenston's daughter, the Hollywood movie star?" I asked.

"The one and only."

"You're telling me Emmy Kenston is a wolf shifter too?"

"She goes to the ARC, an all-shifter college, with my sister Jessie. They're good friends, and according to her Emmy was adopted and had no clue what she was until she shifted for the first time. Fortunately, her parents at least knew of shifters already, which is super rare for humans."

"True story," Lily confirmed. "Only she's not a wolf. She's a squirrel."

"A squirrel? You have got to be shitting me," I blurted out, making them laugh.

"Honey, if there's an animal, at some point in history there was a shifter of that animal spirit."

I shook my head unable to believe what they were telling me.

"You know, this has been quite enlightening," Clara confessed. "We should have another chat soon. I'm sure you'll have dozens more questions the more you learn about it, and it's kind of cool to hear things from your prospective."

Ruby rolled her eyes. "Nerd!"

Peyton scowled at her. "Be nice. See Clara's the scientist of the family and specializes in animals. So of course she's super fascinated by you and the whole shifter human bond thing."

I could tell by the look on Clara's face that there was a lot more to it than that, but I didn't want to put her on the spot by asking.

"I'd love to do this again," I said instead.

"Soon," Lily insisted.

James

Chapter 19

A night away from my mate shouldn't be this difficult. It wasn't that long ago that I'd had a life. I didn't need Katherine every second of every day.

Mine! my wolf growled.

I stopped my pacing and flopped down on the couch.

How the hell did I let it escalate this quickly?

For years the anxiety and need to be near her was a constant in my life, but not like this. This was so much worse.

The upside to being back with her was getting to sleep in an actual bed in my skin, but all that time in my fur had been worth it to keep the negative side of an unrequited mating bond at bay.

The fact that she wasn't fighting this and seemed to be taking everything in stride amazed me. She was incredible. I don't know how I would have handled learning that shifters existed and lived all around me. With Hollywood's depictions of our kind or the monsters they seemed to love that were similar to my kind, I probably would have shit myself.

I still hated that I'd shifted so suddenly in front of her as a first exposure. I should have talked to her first, but I'd been so shocked to find out about the baby that I hadn't even thought, I'd just acted.

Hearing the unmistakable sound of tires on my gravel driveway made me groan.

I didn't want company, but I also knew those assholes weren't going to give me any choice.

I rarely ever locked my door, and they knew it. Without a knock of warning, my front door opened and one by one my friends walked in.

"All six of us together three times in a month? What do I owe for the honor of this?"

Austin laughed as he looked down at me still laid out on the couch.

"Well, he's not pacing," he teased.

"But he was," Clay pointed out the track I'd walked across the carpet.

I sighed. "What do you assholes want?"

"Just checking in on you," Emmett said, pushing my legs off the couch and taking a seat.

Wyatt set down a cooler and pulled out a beer to hand to me.

"Girls are out tonight, we figured you could use the company, pops."

I groaned. They all knew about the baby.

"How's your wolf holding up?" Clay asked.

"It's been years of being just close enough to her to keep my shit together, but this is so much bigger and different now. I hate having her out of my sight. I feel like I'm losing it."

There was no sense in lying to them. These were my boys. They were here to help me and no matter what happened in life, they would always be Team James.

"It's the baby," Thomas said. "I mean, Lily and I are mated and secure in our relationship, but it doesn't stop my wolf from going apeshit every time she's pregnant."

"Which is always," Austin said with a snort.

Thomas just grinned.

"You should be so lucky," he shot back.

Austin scowled and shook his head. "No thank you. I like being my own man. I'm in no rush to find a mate."

Emmett shrugged. "I wouldn't mind it. I think it would be nice to find my mate. I've been dating again, but it's hard watching you guys find your true mates and be willing to settle for second place."

"It's worth the wait," Wyatt insisted.

"How the hell would you know? You barely even had a wolf when you violated my favorite cousin," Austin insisted.

Wyatt just grinned used to Austin's jabs by now.

"She was worth it, even if it means I have to listen to you run your mouth about it for the rest of my life."

"I don't think I could have settled," Clay admitted.

"Katherine's human," I blurted out. "Yeah, okay, you guys already know that, but I've known she was meant to be mine for years."

"I remember you dating her years ago. How the hell have you survived not claiming her all this time?" Emmett asked.

They all stopped the teasing and cutting up and watched me closely.

I sighed. Of course they'd ask.

"I have spent almost every night since sleeping in my fur under her porch."

They stared at me blinking with blank expressions on their faces before exploding in laughter.

"That's pathetic!"

"No way."

"I don't believe it."

"Did it work?"

Thomas was the only one who didn't react because I'd already confessed that much to him.

"Make fun all you want, but it kept his wolf sane through all of this. It's kind of a miracle if you ask me," he defended me.

"Maybe it's not as strong since she's human."

I growled and fur immediately started sprouting up my arms.

"Or not," Austin retracted his statement quickly.

I felt Thomas's Alpha powers wash over me, and my wolf snapped at him in protest as I fought to regain control.

"Don't question his bond with her," he warned them all. "She may be human, but their bond is strong and flowing freely between them. It's not one-sided."

My heart leapt in my chest.

"You can feel that?" I asked.

He nodded. "Alpha perks. It's kind of a way for me to know for sure if it's a true mate bond. There can be a bond, even a strong one, between compatible mates, but that usually takes time and happens after a full mating. The true mate bond is always there. I just have to be in the same room with both partners to feel it."

"Cool."

"You're turning into a freaking sap, James," Austin teased.

I just shrugged, unaffected by his jab. When it came to Katherine, I didn't care. Never had, never would. I didn't want her to ever question my love for her.

"You're in love with her, aren't you?" Emmett said.

I laughed. "I've never loved anyone else. It's always been her."

"I didn't even know you ever dated her, or anyone really," Austin confessed. "But remember when Peyton and Ollie were battling his ex for custody of Eve, and that bitch tried to drag CPS into it?"

I nodded. I never forgot a single encounter I'd ever had with my woman.

"Well, I knew there was something there. I didn't press it, which isn't like me, I know." He smirked. "But it was like this tangible thing in the room, and I saw the way you looked at her."

"We didn't just date," I confessed. "We were practically living together. I even got down on one knee, ring and all, to ask her to marry me. I didn't think I could tell her about what I was, so I opted for the human expression instead."

"You're an idiot," Austin said. "At some point you'd have claimed her, and then what? Oh honey, I'm so sorry I bit you. Can you bite me back? I mean, can she? Are you doomed to have a one-sided bond because she doesn't have the proper equipment to seal it? Have you even thought about any of this?"

"Of course I've thought about this. She's my mate. I don't know how this shit works, but I know she's mine. The rest we're just going to have to figure out along the way. I never imagined we'd involve a kid. I have literally never let myself think about having a child because of this and knowing how hard of a time half-breeds can have in a pack. But we're here now and it's happening. I will do whatever I have to do to protect my mate and our child."

"Calm down," Thomas said, letting his Alpha powers flow over me again. "We expect nothing less. And right here, right now, we're making a pact to support you through this no matter what. Your child will have the full protection and security of the Six Pack. Are you with me, guys?"

"Hell yes! This little one has some fierce uncles who will destroy anyone who tries to make him or her feel less than normal for being a half-breed," Emmett said fiercely.

Clay nodded. "We protect our own."

"Our family," Wyatt added.

"I'm in and I'm going to spoil the shit out of this kid," Austin announced.

I wasn't an overly emotional guy, but pride welled up within me as I nodded. This was my family, my chosen family. They would always have my back and I knew without a doubt that no matter what happened, they'd take care of my kid too.

"Thanks, guys. I, uh, whew. I don't even know what to say to this."

"Well don't be a pansy and make it awkward or anything," Austin teased. "This is the power of the Six Pack right here."

"Austin's right. And it goes without saying that the Pack will stand behind you too. Make it permanent and I'll personally see to it that Katherine is granted full Pack privileges just like any other Collier mate."

"Wow. Thomas, are you sure about that? You could catch some shit for granting that to a human, mate or not."

"I'm aware and I'm sure. Claim her already."

I grinned. "That is the plan."

The rest of the night we just hung out like old times, drinking beer and cutting up. I was overwhelmingly grateful for each of them. I couldn't even imagine my life without them in it.

At one point in my life, I would have walked away from them, the Pack, all of it. I would have turned my back on everything I am just to be with Katherine. But now, I felt like the luckiest son-of-bitch in the world because I didn't have to.

Freaking out and shifting in front of her, forcing me to explain everything, just might have been the best thing I've ever done.

Everyone stayed until Lily returned Katherine to me.

They walked in the door laughing and then stopped when they saw us all there and the stack of beers piled into a pyramid on the table. We weren't exactly drunk, having run out of beer an hour ago, but I knew what it looked like.

"You have got to be kidding me. I thought you were watching the girls tonight," Lily scolded Thomas.

He just shrugged. "James needed us. You stole his mate. Plus, Mom volunteered."

She just glared at him.

"I'm coming. I rode over with Emmett, so you can drive me home."

I rose when he did. We all did.

Thomas gave me a hug. "We'll talk soon," he assured me, before saying goodbye to each of the others and then walking over to give Lily a kiss. "Did you have a good time at least?"

She softened immediately as she shared a look with Katherine that I didn't fully understand.

"It was certainly informative," she said.

"What does that mean?" I asked.

My question only sent the girls into a fit of giggles as they hugged one another before Lily grabbed Thomas's hand and said goodnight.

I couldn't help how happy it made me feel to see my mate embrace Thomas's mate. It gave me hope in a way I'd never experienced before.

The others followed their lead and said goodbye. They each took a second to give Katherine a hug and talk to her for a minute before leaving.

"So that's the Six Pack, huh?" she asked. "I mean I've met them, but not quite like this. I didn't know they were coming over tonight."

"Me either." I chuckled. "They were worried about me, knowing you were away tonight."

Her brow furrowed.

"Um, was it hard on you to be away?"

"Yes," I said. "Harder than I expected."

"Me, too. It was so weird. I mean I had a great time, and I'm glad I went. They answered a lot of questions I had, and it was nice to know I wasn't entirely losing my mind. But I was also anxious, like I wanted to get back here soon. I actually asked to leave a little early. They all assured me that was normal. It doesn't feel normal, James."

I went to her and wrapped her in my arms.

"I can feel our bond growing stronger. Plus with the baby, I think it just has my wolf on edge."

"I think I have an imaginary wolf then, because she's on edge too."

I snickered. She was adorable trying to relate to everything.

When she yawned, I felt a slight stab of disappointment, but it had been a long day and I knew she needed more rest than usual while she was carrying my pup.

I grinned.

It still didn't feel entirely real. She was pregnant with my child.

"What are you smiling about?"

I gave her a quick peck on the lips and then let my hand splay out across her still flat stomach.

"I'm just in awe of you. I can't believe there's a little being in there that we made."

She melted in my arms.

"You're really happy about this?"

"I couldn't be happier, babe. I never allowed myself to think about being a dad, but now that this is happening, I'm just so excited for our future."

Katherine
Chapter 20

I gulped hard hearing his words. James was genuinely happy about this baby, while I was still in shock and maybe in a tiny bit of denial. It wasn't real to me yet. Mostly, if I let myself really think about it, I started to freak out.

"You look tired. Ready for bed?"

I nodded. "I have work in the morning, James. I should probably go home."

"Yeah, we haven't really talked about that yet, have we?"

I shook my head.

"Are you more comfortable at your house?"

"It's not that," I assured him. "Really. And after talking to the girls, I get why you would want to live in Pack territory, it's just, all my stuff is still there, and I have to be in court early tomorrow morning. That's it. I promise."

"It's not that. I don't care where we live, as long as you don't shut me out again."

The pain and desperation in his voice nearly took me to my knees.

"I'm not," I said quickly to reassure him. "I really do have an early morning. If you aren't on call, pack your stuff and stay with me. Inside, in my bed, to be clear. Not under my porch. That shall now be used for banishment only if you seriously piss me off."

He laughed when I grinned. It looked like a weight was lifted from his shoulders.

"You're sure?"

"We're in this together, right? Wolves mate for life."

That thought was still a little terrifying, but more so when I wasn't standing before James saying it here. Here, it felt like the rightest thing I'd ever said.

Plus, there was the added benefit of the huge smile taking over his face as he leaned in and kissed me.

"I love you so much, Katherine. Thank you for being so understanding about everything."

I scowled, remembering earlier, and he immediately picked up on it.

"What is it?"

"I met Brady tonight. He's not very trusting of humans. I doubt he'll be the only one unhappy with me being here."

He sighed. "Brady has his reasons. He's also a half-breed."

I flinched at the word.

"I know, I don't like it either, but it is a fact. So are his brothers, and one of his nieces. And he couldn't love any of them more. It's a mixed bag of emotions for him. But that's his issue, his demons, not ours."

I nodded in understanding.

"Babe, if you aren't comfortable living in the Pack, I will commute. I have a commitment to Collier and while I will always choose you and our little family first, I truly hope it doesn't come to that."

"You just want your cake and to eat it too," I teased as I wrapped my arms around his neck and kissed him.

He smiled against my lips, and I could suddenly feel his happiness. It made me smile too.

"I can feel when you're genuinely happy. Did you know that?" I asked, pulling back to look into his eyes.

"You can?"

I nodded. "Is that bad?"

"No. That's amazing."

I quirked my head to the side as I studied him. "That makes you happy?"

"Very."

He gave me another quick kiss. "I never imagined you would feel so much, too."

"So you can feel my emotions?"

"Yes. I have been able to for a long time. It's why I started growling when that asshole kissed you at the end of your date. I could feel your discomfort and had to step in and do something about it."

I knew the exact moment with Allen he was talking about. "I'm glad you did. My guardian wolf. My hero."

His arms held me a little tighter as he kissed me again.

"Come on," he finally conceded. "Let me grab my uniform and we'll head home. Because I can also feel how tired you are."

"Surprising you with anything is going to be difficult, isn't it?"

"Maybe, but it's okay. You already gave me the surprise of a lifetime when you told me you were pregnant."

"Right. I'm pregnant."

"Still freaks you out too?"

"It does. This certainly wasn't planned."

Worry shot through me, and I realized quickly it wasn't me, it was him. That was going to take some getting used to.

"Are you not happy about the baby?"

"James, I'm still in shock. I mean, I find out I'm pregnant with an unplanned baby by my ex-boyfriend that I hadn't really seen or spent time with in years except a random one-night stand out of the blue. And then I discover he's not quite human and shifts into a wolf. A wolf! That should terrify me, but it doesn't. Still, I'm just trying to process everything. It's a lot."

"I know. You're doing great."

He rubbed my shoulders and then disappeared to grab his stuff.

"I'll follow you home since we'll need both cars tomorrow."

"Yeah, okay."

I looked around his house. It was a nice place, and I could be happy living there, but logistically we just weren't there yet. Still, I was grateful he wasn't leaving me alone to deal with all of this. I'd have to at some point, but for now, I was just happy to have his unwavering support.

The drive home alone may have been a mistake though. It was giving me time to let things sink in some and by the time I pulled into my driveway I was bordering on hysteria thinking through everything that was happening and how it would affect my future.

James parked and jumped out of his car to practically rip my driver's side door off. He looked a little wild in the eyes as they darted around the yard looking for a threat.

"What's wrong?" he demanded.

I burst into tears, and I didn't even understand why.

Lily and the girls had warned me it would happen, not that it could, but that it absolutely would.

"I don't know," I wailed.

"Is the baby okay? Are you hurt?"

The fact that his first concern was our child and me made my heart swell with happiness as I smiled up at him through my tears.

"I'm fine," I said. It wasn't entirely a lie. "Just a bit weepy and emotional."

"Oh, like the pregnancy hormones stuff?"

I nodded. "I think so."

He took a deep breath and nodded. "Okay, yeah. Those can be insane. I've seen Lily freak out over the slightest little things. I can deal with this," he said, as if he were giving himself a little pep talk.

It was so cute, it made me cry a little more.

I blew out a sharp breath.

"Can we just go inside and go to bed. I think I need sleep."

He swooped me up in his arms and carried me up the porch stairs and into the house like I didn't weigh a thing. Despite my protests, he didn't stop until he gently laid me down on the bed.

"I can walk, you know."

"But why? You needed to get to bed quickly. It's the least I could do."

"James, you aren't carrying me around for the next nine months."

"No, but occasionally, when you need it the most. I'll give you a few minutes to get ready for bed. I'll be in the kitchen if you need me."

He left, closing the door behind him and I laid there with my mouth slightly ajar in shock.

He remembered.

When we were practically living together the last time, I always asked for a little me time just before bed. I didn't have to ask now, he remembered.

I got up and stripped out of my clothes, then went to shower, trying to let go of my heightened emotions. By the time I dried my hair and crawled into bed, I was exhausted.

My eyes were just starting to drift shut, even though my mind was still whirling, when the door opened and he crept inside.

I looked up just in time to see him set a cup down on the nightstand next to me.

"Chamomile, right?"

Tears welled up in my eyes once more.

"You remembered?"

He shrugged. "There's nothing I don't remember when it comes to you, babe."

His words warmed me more than the hot tea as I sipped it.

He stripped down to his boxers and slid under the covers next to me. Boy was he in for a surprise. I'd been so tired I hadn't even bothered with pajamas.

His hand stilled on my hip as he realized it.

I smiled around the cup as I took another sip of tea.

"We're sleeping naked now?"

I laughed. "I'm so tired, I didn't even bother to get dressed."

"Hell yes."

He jumped up and took off his boxers before crawling back in, but not before I got an eyeful of him long, hard, and ready.

I groaned.

"Sleep, James. We're going to sleep."

"I know," he said innocently, as if I hadn't noticed his dick at full attention.

True to his word though, he ignored his own needs. When I finished my tea, I was already feeling much more relaxed, but when he wrapped me up in his arms and I laid my head on his chest, my whole body melted, and I drifted off quickly into the best sleep I'd had in years.

*****

The next morning, I awoke, stretching, feeling like I'd had the weirdest dream of my life. My whole body stiffened when I realized I wasn't alone.

James.

I could smell his delicious scent surround me even though he was still snoring softly.

It wasn't a dream. It was all real.

I laid there staring at him sleeping as I really let my new reality sink in. I'd been overwhelmed and emotional last night, but this morning in a whole new light, everything felt right.

There were no guarantees I wouldn't freak out and have a complete meltdown eventually, but for now, I was okay, happy even. If I had to find myself unexpectedly pregnant, I couldn't imagine a better man by my side for it.

He wouldn't leave me alone to deal with any of this, not that his wolf would let him, but also, because he wouldn't want to miss a single moment of it, and I knew that to be true with my whole heart.

Overwhelmed with gratitude and love, or maybe lust as I studied him, I let my hands roam across his body. It was so perfectly familiar, though harder and more matured than when we were younger. I tried to memorize every little change as I unabashedly explored him.

I knew by the way the sheets were tented that he was still hard.

Licking my lips, I smiled as I crawled down his body under the covers. I wasn't sure there was such a thing as a beautiful dick, but if there was, that award went to James, my mate.

I fought back giggles just thinking it, but plenty of dirty thoughts flashed through my mind, making me instantly horny.

I moaned as I swirled my tongue around him. His salty taste never bothered me. He had always been such a generous lover that it excited me to give him back a little.

Licking him up and down before I sucked him deep into the back of my throat, I started stroking him with my hand while bobbing my head up and down.

His whole body came alive with a jolt.

"What the…"

He pulled back the covers and looked down at me. I smiled when our eyes met, letting my teeth lightly graze him.

He cursed and closed his eyes.

I could feel him growing impossibly harder by the second.

In a sudden move, the covers were jerked from my body and I found myself being lifted and settled on top of him, straddling his body. He penetrated me in one smooth stroke as I sat there in shock, letting my body adjust to the full mass of him.

Then I moved, making myself moan.

There was a wild look in his eyes that delighted me as he grabbed my hips and thrust upwards. It didn't take long for my surprise to wear off and my body to get on board as I rode him hard, seeking my own pleasure as much as his.

He touched me in all the right places, pulling my body closer and closer to climax.

But when he growled, my whole body tightened in response as I let go, over the cliff in a deep dive dragging him right there with me.

Gasping for breath, I collapsed down onto his chest and kissed him all over.

"Damn. That was some wakeup call," he finally said when he found his voice again.

James
Chapter 21

I walked into work with a smile on my face that I couldn't contain.

"Someone's in a surprisingly good mood this morning," Julian commented.

"Yeah, he got laid," Ryder said after glancing up from the stack of papers he was working on.

"Nice change after the last few weeks," Deaton added.

"Shut up and get back to work," I barked, but there was no malice behind it because they were all right.

I walked into my office and shut the door.

Damn, I felt great this morning. Everything was going so well. It felt like a dream come true. After years of pining, Katherine was finally mine. Sure, I still had to explain a few things about the actual details of how we would seal our bond, but I couldn't let myself think about that now, or the fact that I had no idea how it would actually work with her being a human.

Thomas had once told me that God didn't make mistakes when matching mates. It was apparently something Lily's mother was known for saying. I had to believe it was true, and if it was, then I didn't have to stress the details because he wouldn't pair me with a mate that couldn't reciprocate and seal our bond.

Somehow it would all work out… it had to.

I had a lot to catch up on, but mostly just paperwork. My deputies had done a great job of holding down the fort during my personal crisis.

I chuckled.

Why the hell did I ever think staying away from her was the right thing to do?

I shook my head, a little disgusted with myself. I'd had everything so wrong.

None of that mattered now because she knew all my secrets and we were having a baby. Nothing in this world would keep me from my mate now.

I didn't even mind the workload ahead of me as I started to dig out of the paperwork pile threatening to bury me. It was all done with a smile on my face.

Around noon my stomach started to growl, and I knew it was time for a break.

My cell phone rang, and I picked it up, grinning when I saw Katherine's picture flash across the screen. It was an old one and I made a mental note to update it soon.

"Hey babe."

"Are you busy?"

"No, I was just slowing down to break for lunch. You aren't free, are you?"

"Um, no, I'm not. Sorry. I'll be in court much of the day and have a few home checks to make this evening, so I'll be late getting home tonight."

"Alright, your house or mine?"

"Um, mine, I guess. I don't have anything out in Collier until Wednesday."

"Out in Collier? What's going on here?"

"Just going through some old files that we were blocked on due to jurisdictional issues. I would really like to get them closed out so it's just a couple of minor well-checks. I don't imagine anything will come of all it, now that I know, well, you know."

"Okay, well, if you need me to escort you around, let me know. They still aren't going to be okay with you snooping around just because you're in the know now."

"I get that, and I already had these lined up before that. I gave them a two-week notice. And yes, I would love it if you would tag along."

"Great. I'll mark Wednesday off on my calendar then."

"And how about dinner tomorrow night? Can you make that?"

She was quiet on the other end for a minute, and I could sense her nervousness despite the miles between us. It made me smile, as that was a sign that our bond really was strengthening.

"It's with my parents," she blurted out. "We have to tell them."

I gulped hard.

Her parents?

I had to tell Judge Carter that I'd gone and knocked up his only daughter.

I thought I might be sick at the idea.

"James? Hello?"

"Yeah, I'm here. Tomorrow? Okay."

"Are you? Are you okay? Something feels… I don't know, off."

"No, it's fine. Just a momentary reality check. I guess we should plan to tell my family sometime soon too."

"Right. I hadn't thought about that. I've never even met your family, James."

"I know. I'm sorry about that. You will soon. I promise."

"Are you sure you're okay?"

"Fine. Just trying not to think the worst about how your father is going to react by the news."

She laughed. "He's going to freak out and then when he finds out it's you that knocked me up, he's going to be thrilled. Trust me on that. My dad is still like your biggest fan and gives me shit all the time for having dumped you."

"I knew I liked your dad for a reason."

"Shut up. Tomorrow night then? I can tell Mom to make it for four."

"I wouldn't miss it."

"Great. So, my house tonight?"

"I'll pick up dinner at Kate's on my way in since you said it might be a late night."

"Perfect. Thanks."

"Love you," I said as we were ending the call.

She sighed happily on the other end.

"I love you too. See you tonight."

There was such a comfortable familiarity how that conversation ended.

I loved her. I'd always loved her, but I was truly and unquestionably in love with her.

It hit me hard that this was our second chance at making it work. I couldn't screw this up, no matter what. Katherine was my world and I wanted more than anything to build my life with her.

I got up and walked over to the tall file cabinet in the corner. Squatting down I unlocked the bottom drawer and pulled out the small box I kept in the back of it.

I rolled the box over in my hands and then slowly opened it with a grin.

The last time I saw that ring inside I'd been devastated. We hadn't been ready then. I knew that now, but this time things were different. We had a kid on the way, and it would go a long way with her family and human life to wear this ring.

My gut twisted in nerves at the idea of asking her again.

This time would be different. I had to believe that after everything we were going through. I shoved it in my pocket, knowing that I was going to be needing it soon.

I opened my office door and yelled out, "Hey, anyone ordering in for lunch today?"

"Ryder just left to go pick up pizza," Julian informed me.

"Can you call in an extra meat lovers for me and have him bring it back with him?"

"Sure thing. I'm on it."

With that settled, I dove back into my work. The only interruption I had all day was when Ryder delivered my pizza. It was almost unsettling how quiet it was. By the end of the day, I was almost beginning to get paranoid.

The guys had been checking in on me so frequently that it seemed weird not to hear from any of them today.

Right at five I locked up, knowing the rest of my work could wait, and said goodbye. I drove home and packed a larger bag than I had taken last night before making my way to Kate's Diner.

The place was busy for the dinner rush, so I took a seat at the bar.

Kate smiled when she saw me.

"Be over in a second."

Austin was pitching in and beat her to it.

"How'd it go today?" he asked.

"Good. I'm about halfway through the mess of paperwork I ignored the last few weeks."

"That's good. How's Katherine?"

"She's fine. Won't be home until late."

"And where exactly is home these days?"

I shrugged. "Here and there. We're sort of bouncing back and forth at the moment."

"Eventually you're going to have to settle on just one."

"I'm aware, and we will. We don't need to rush that though."

"Is she going to be okay living in Pack territory?"

"I don't know," I told him honestly. "But her house is less than twenty minutes by car or six point three miles in fur from mine, so it's not that big of a deal if she isn't. I'll still be around the area regardless."

"I'm not even going to ask how you know exactly the mileage in fur."

"Best path there is," I grinned. "Look, I'm just saying that regardless of where we decide to live, you aren't getting rid of me."

He frowned. "Not the same."

"Austin, I'm going to do what's best for my family. That's what's important."

"I know. I just hate thinking of you living outside of the Pack."

"I'll cross that bridge when I get there. Now, what's the special today?"

"Peyton's baked spaghetti with salad and garlic bread."

"Great, I'll take two to go."

My tone must have told him I was done with this conversation because he just walked away shaking his head.

Things were going good for me right now. I sure as hell wasn't going to invite trouble by pressing her to make big decisions like that anytime soon.

When our to-go order was ready, I paid and said goodbye. He was too busy to really notice or care anyway.

Once home, I set out our dinner on the small kitchen table and then took a moment to look around the house. Honestly, very little had changed. My pictures were no longer around the house, but that was an easy thing to remedy, and it only took me two drawers to find a whole stack of them.

I grinned, realizing that she probably couldn't bring herself to toss them out. There were subtle signs like that everywhere, telling me she really did feel our bond too.

Why had I been so pigheaded? All she'd ever done was ask to slow things down and give her a little space. I'd overreacted and given her all the space in the world, well, as far as she knew.

In truth, I'd never strayed far from my mate. I'd seen the damage an unrequited bond could have on a person, and it terrified me. Staying close to her, even if she didn't know it, had kept me sane. I was certain of it.

Just as certain as I was that if it happened again and she tried to push me away, it wouldn't work this time. I was all in and there was no turning back again. I didn't just need to be near her, I needed her.

By the time the clock struck seven and she still wasn't home, it took everything in my power not to call and check on her. My wolf and I conjured up a million different horrible scenarios that could happen to her out there in the world, alone, unprotected.

For a shifter, a pregnant female was the most precious and vulnerable thing in the world. It made even the strongest of us fall prey to uncertainty and paranoia. They couldn't shift and protect themselves during the gestational period.

I was aware that Katherine would always be more vulnerable as a human, but even knowing that didn't stop the additional craziness that came with a pregnancy. As everything about our situation was starting to sink in, that reality was glaringly obvious to me. It's what had changed the most. That was the thing drawing me irrevocably closer to her.

As my anxiety spiked, I began pacing her living room floor back and forth, back and forth. It wasn't a good sign for the state of my wolf or me, but I couldn't seem to stop myself.

By the time her car pulled up and she walked into the house, I had worked myself up into a near blind rage. My body was shaking, and I was stuck in a sort of half skin, half fur state. I didn't want her to see me like that, but I couldn't drag myself from it.

When Katherine walked in and saw me, she screamed and dropped her bag to the floor. Still, I couldn't pull myself together.

"James, what's wrong?" she whispered.

When I didn't respond, she grabbed her phone and dialed a number.

"Lily? I just got home and James is sort of half himself and sprouting a lot of fur. He's pacing the living room and doesn't look like he fully sees me. What the hell should I do?... You want me to do what?... I trust you... You're sure about this?... Okay. Hurry!"

She turned back to me, and I could smell fear rolling off of her which only signaled to my wolf that something was wrong and he needed to protect her. Even though I was somewhat aware that it was me that she was afraid of, I just couldn't fully rationalize what needed to happen to fix the situation.

"Okay, it's just me. Lily says I should talk to you and um, go to you. She promises you can't hurt me. Could you maybe not look so scary and please don't eat me. Here goes."

As she stepped closer with her hand out between us, my wolf took notice. I watched her slowly approach us until her hand touched my chest.

"Mate," I said in a strange voice as I grabbed her arm and crushed her to me.

She screamed and tried to jerk back as I wrapped my arms around her and breathed in her scent. My entire world righted itself once more as I regained control with a violent shudder.

As my fur disappeared and my body shook, Katherine embraced me back.

"It's okay," she said. "I'm here and I'm fine. I just got tied up at work and guess I should have called. It's been a while since I've done the relationship thing, but I'll try to remember next time. Are you okay?"

I nodded. Nuzzling my nose into the crook of her neck, I forced my canines to rescind. I couldn't exactly claim her right now. She was terrified of me and that bothered me more than anything.

"I'm sorry," I whispered when I finally found my voice. "I'm so sorry."

I was just starting to calm down when I heard footsteps running up the stairs and the door burst open.

In one smooth motion, I pushed Katherine safely behind me and growled at the intruder.

"Calm down!" I heard, seconds before I was hit with a powerful surge of Alpha powers.

"It's okay. Back it down a notch, Thomas. She's already got him under control."

"Control? He growled at me."

"You barged into my house unannounced," I argued.

"Katherine, are you okay?" Lily asked.

She nodded.

Thomas looked around and shook his head.

"Rough evening?"

I blew out a breath. "I guess you could say that."

"It's all perfectly normal. Mating males get quite territorial and obnoxiously protective, but so do soon-to-be fathers, and right now, that boy is both. Everything within him is telling him to protect you every second of every day. It does get better, I promise. He's just feeling a lot possessive right now," Lily explained to Katherine.

A part of me expected her to freak out and run, demand I leave, or something equally horrible. Those concerns still had my wolf on edge.

"What can I do to make it easier for him?" she surprised me by asking.

Lily grinned. "Great question. So you're still all in?"

"Of course I am. He didn't hurt me in any way, he just scared me a little."

Her being defensive of me and wanting to help me calmed me more than probably anything else could have. I hadn't blown it. She was still here, and she wasn't leaving.

I was fully aware that Thomas was watching me closely, but as I started to settle, so did he.

"Are you okay?" he finally asked.

"No, but I will be."

"Katherine, are you okay?" he asked my mate.

"She'll be fine," Lily said.

I couldn't help but smile a little at how protective my Pack Mother had already become of my mate.

"I hate to interfere here," Thomas started.

"Then don't," I warned.

He side-eyed me and continued. "But I think it would be best if you two stayed in territory for the time being. I think having the scent of Pack surrounding him just might help some."

"Do you really think that would help?" Katherine asked Lily.

She nodded. "Probably. I mean he's going to be a bit unstable until you seal your bond, and even then, until the baby is born. It's a lot all at once for him."

I hated the way they were talking about me as if I weren't right here.

"Okay then, I'll pack up a bag and we'll stay at his house tonight instead."

"No," I protested. "You're tired and need to eat still. We can just stay here."

Lily and Thomas shared a look that made me want to elbow him in the gut. Even in this heightened state I knew that wasn't appropriate when he was in Alpha mode like this.

"It's okay," Katherine said as she walked over and hugged me. "If it will make things easier for you then it's fine."

"Okay," I said softly.

"What's for dinner? I'm starving."

"Baked spaghetti on the table and waiting."

It made me feel good to provide for her.

"Will you two stay for dinner?" she asked them.

"No, we already ate and have to get back home to get the girls ready for bed," Lily insisted.

"I'm really sorry I dragged you both out here."

"It's fine. Always call. I'm serious. Even if you just need to talk or have a question, always call me," Lily assured her.

"We'll have dinner and head back to my house," I assured Thomas. "Um, thanks for watching out for her tonight."

"We're here for you too, asshole," he affectionately told me.

I nodded, still feeling a little off, but better.

Once they were gone, I noticed Katherine walking around touching the pictures of us I'd put back out around the house.

"Where did you find these?"

"In a drawer. Sorry. It's sort of my way of marking my territory."

She nodded like she understood and then shrugged.

"Better than peeing on the place."

I barked out a laugh.

"Don't try to deny it, the girls told me the other night that it was a possibility."

I looked down at the ground unable to meet her eyes.

"You didn't!"

"I don't know what you're talking about. Sit down and eat already. I can hear your stomach grumbling."

"When? Where?" she asked even as she obeyed and sat down to eat.

"Fine. It's just around your property line to warn off any stray wolves in the area. It's not a big deal."

"When?"

"Does it matter?"

"When James?"

I sighed, knowing she wasn't going to let it go. "Once a month I make my rounds. Are you satisfied."

She laughed, letting the last of her worries float away.

"It's not a big deal. It's just a wolf thing."

She continued to laugh and then stopped.

"Wait, you wouldn't do that in the house. You are housebroken, right?"

I groaned as I glared at her, sending her into another fit of giggles.

Katherine
Chapter 22

Nothing felt righter than waking up in James's arms.

"Good morning, beautiful," he said in a sexy sleepy voice.

"Good morning. What's your day look like today?"

He shrugged as he stretched.

"Nothing major, just paperwork. Hopefully it will stay that way."

"Well don't jinx it. We have dinner with my parents, remember?"

"I know. I'll be there."

"Good, because we have to tell them about the baby. I booked my first prenatal visit yesterday and it's a small town, James. I feel like I'm on a ticking time-bomb waiting to see if the gossip train reaches it first. I do not want my parents to know before I have a chance to tell them."

"You could always use Doc."

"Doc? Who's that?"

"Our Pack physician."

"Um, okay," I said with a million questions going through my mind. "So, don't hate me for asking this, but is Doc an actual doctor?"

He looked at me like I was crazy.

"Of course. What else would he be?"

"Umm, a veterinarian?"

He groaned and rolled over to pin me to the bed.

"What? How am I supposed to know? It's a legit question."

"I know."

He hesitated and I knew there was more.

"What aren't you telling me?"

"He's both. But only because he pitches in around the ranch when needed too."

I cracked up laughing and he started tickling me.

"James, stop! I'm going to pee myself."

I pushed him from me, jumped up, and ran for the bathroom. I could still hear him chuckling in the other room.

Somehow, we managed to get through the rest of the morning and go about our separate ways for work.

"You're going to be okay?" I asked, hesitant to leave him after last night.

"I'm fine, babe. I'm sorry I freaked you out like that. I'm okay, though."

"Five o'clock sharp at my parents' house, got it?"

"I got it. I'll be there. Or would you rather I meet up with you and we go together."

I considered that but knowing the day I had ahead of me, it was probably best if we just meet there.

"Just meet me there. You remember how to get there?"

"I've got it. Have a great day."

He kissed me, making me wish I could just lock the door and stay right there in his arms.

"Go, before I change my mind."

I hesitated.

"Is that a threat or a promise?"

He laughed, smacked me on the ass to get me moving, and then escorted me to his car. He was already dressed in his uniform for the day and looked so handsome.

"Why do I find it so hard to leave you? It's just work."

He smiled happily.

"It's the bond. I feel it too."

With one last kiss, I drove off with a million new thoughts running through my head.

The bond? Was the bond controlling us? How was I supposed to know if this was what I really wanted or just what this ridiculous bond thing was telling me I wanted? I needed to know more about it, and I knew Lily was just the person to ask.

I made a personal reminder to call her the second I got a break in my day.

Unfortunately, that never happened.

My day was hectic from start to finish. By the time it was time to call it quits and head over to my parents' house, I was utterly exhausted.

Sitting in their driveway, I called James.

"Shit. It's five already?"

"Not quite. Is everything okay?"

"No. I'm going to be late. I'm sorry. We had an incident out on the range. I can't even believe you got through to me."

The line had lots of static, making it hard to hear him, but I was making out most of it.

"Well, it's okay. Do what you need to do."

I was disappointed, but I understood. How many cases had dragged me out at all hours of the night. He was Sheriff of Collier. He had an important job and I needed to be supportive of that.

"I'll try to wrap things up and get there as soon as I can."

"Great. And if not, it's okay, James. Really."

"Thanks. And again, I'm sorry. Love you."

"Love you too."

I could hear someone yelling for him in the background when the line cut off.

As I walked into the house, I was kind of glad I hadn't quite worked up the nerve to tell Mom to plan for four tonight. She always overcooked so I knew it wouldn't be an issue. Maybe a part of me had just been waiting for him to let me down.

That's not fair, I chastised myself.

I knew fully well how important his job was. I was just scared to face my parents alone. I wasn't good at keeping things from them, and right now, I was harboring a lot of secrets, most of which weren't mine to tell.

"Katherine is that you?" Mom yelled.

"Well, who else would it be?" Dad asked her.

They both hurried out of the kitchen to greet me.

I had certainly scored in the parent department. They'd raised me to be independent while also loving and spoiling me in the process. I adored them and prayed I'd handle parenthood as graciously as these two had.

The thought made me a little weepy as my eyes misted over.

Dad hugged me. "What's wrong, sweetie?"

"Nothing. Just a long day," I assured him.

"You look pale, Katherine. Are you okay? Doesn't she look a little pale to you?"

"She's fine. You look beautiful. Your mom made our favorite tonight. Broiled fish with lobster sauce."

My stomach rumbled. Then as we walked into the kitchen and the smell of the meal hit me, a wave of nausea had me smacking my hand over my mouth and running for the bathroom. I couldn't get there fast enough.

I dropped to my knees over the toilet and threw up. It just kept coming and wouldn't stop.

"I told you she looked pale," I heard Mom tell Dad from the doorway as they watched me.

When it finally ran its course, I sat down and leaned against the wall. Dad walked over and flushed the toilet with a grimace.

"I really hope it's not contagious. I have a full docket this week."

I snorted. "Trust me, it's not contagious."

"But how can you be sure? You really should go to the doctor. Maybe I should just call and see if she'll make a house call," Mom fussed.

Dad helped me up and back to the kitchen. The second I smelled the fish I was running for the toilet again. This time, at least there was very little left in my stomach.

"I'm sorry, but the fish has to go. Please, just put it away. We can order pizza or something if you'd like or try again another day."

"Why would pizza be okay, but fish isn't?" Dad asked, but Mom had a look of suspicion on her face as she quietly left to put away the meal she'd so carefully prepared.

This time when Dad helped me up, we went to the living room to sit down instead.

"I'm worried about you. Maybe taking on Collier County in addition to your current load is just too much right now."

"Dad, I'm fine. I promise."

"Throwing up twice is not fine, Katherine. Your mother's right. You should have let her call the doctor."

"Dad. I said I'm fine."

Fortunately, Mom joined us.

"Pizza will arrive in about twenty minutes."

"Pizza?" Dad asked in disgust. "We just had pizza this weekend."

"You'll live," she assured him.

"I'm sorry. Maybe it would be best if I just head home tonight."

"Don't be silly. You'll stay here so your mother and I can keep an eye on you."

"That's not happening," I assured him.

"You're sick. You don't need to be stubborn about this or alone. We can help until you're better."

"That'll take a while," I muttered under my breath.

"What was that dear?" Mom asked.

"Nothing. Just, I appreciate your concern, but I'm fine. I'm not even sick."

Dad looked at me like I was crazy and then leaned in and sniffed.

"What are you doing?"

"I don't smell any alcohol. The only time I'm fine and puking my guts out is when I've had far too much to drink. It's not like you to drink on the job."

"Dad! I'm not drunk."

"Well, if you're not drunk, then you're sick," he insisted.

"No Dad, I'm not either. I'm pregnant," I blurted out.

Mom's hands flew to her mouth in surprise.

"Pregnant?" Dad asked laughing. "Lord almighty. Didn't your mother teach you about the birds and the bees years ago? At least when you were dating James? Dammit, I'm getting too old to handle these things. Look, Katherine, I love you, but there are certain things required for a woman to get pregnant. Mainly a man, of which, last I checked, you don't have. I promise you, you are not pregnant."

"Jesus, Dad. I know all about sex and the birds and the bees. I'm not a complete idiot."

He looked taken back. "I'd never call you an idiot, just a little naïve and inexperienced in this area."

I stared at him, trying to discern if he was being serious or not and when I realized he was, I burst out laughing.

"George, stop being ridiculous. She's not a virgin for Christ's sake."

"But she's not dating anyone, are you? If she were seeing someone, she'd tell us."

"Dad, yes, I'm seeing someone. I am very much pregnant, about eight weeks now by my estimation. I am sorry if that disappoints you, but it's my reality to deal with."

"Oh Katherine. Why didn't you say anything?" Mom asked, moving to sit next to me as she wrapped an arm around my shoulders.

"I was planning to tell you tonight. I haven't even had my first checkup yet."

Dad picked up my left hand and examined it.

"What are you doing?"

"Looking for a ring. Some guy got my baby knocked up and there damn well better be a ring involved."

"Oh George, stop being ridiculous. This is the twenty-first century and we raised her to be a strong, independent woman capable of raising a child on her own."

"Do you even know who the father is?"

I groaned but was saved by the bell as the pizza arrived.

"I've got it," I insisted as they both just sat there in shock. "And yes, I know who the father is," I yelled back at them as I flung open the door.

When I saw James standing there I burst into tears as he wrapped his arms around me.

"I'm so sorry. I got here as fast as I could."

"Is she trying to get knocked up again by the pizza boy now? What the hell is taking so long?"

James stiffened and I wiped my eyes with a groan.

He started to move, but I put two hands against his chest to stop him.

"They're in shock. I got sick from the smell of fish and it just all came out."

"Uh, did someone order a pizza?" a voice behind him said.

We both turned to see the pizza boy standing there. I gave him the tip I'd almost tried to hand to James when I had opened the door originally, and James took the pizza from him.

"Stay calm. We'll get through this."

"Are you telling me or yourself that?"

"I'm not sure. Both?"

He kissed my temple reassuringly.

"Whatever happens, we face it together, okay?"

"Okay," I said, nodding and grateful to let him take control of the situation.

James walked in ahead of me carrying the pizza like a peace offering.

"James? Well, this is a surprise," Mom said.

"You're delivering pizzas now?" Dad asked.

"Dad," I warned.

"What? Your ex-boyfriend shows up after all these years holding a pizza in my house right when you tell us..."

He stopped as his head whipped back and forth between the two of us noting my close proximity and hand on James's arm.

"James?" his voice boomed throughout the room. "This is the sonofabitch that got you pregnant?"

"George!" Mom exclaimed. Then she leaned over and whispered. "I thought we were still Team James."

"Well, this changes things. What kind of man gets my daughter pregnant and doesn't man up and ask her to marry him?"

"I'm getting around to it. We're both still a little shocked and dealing with the baby news. This wasn't exactly planned," James surprised us all by confessing.

"So you what? Just rekindled an old flame and oops, she's pregnant?"

"Yeah Dad, actually, that's pretty much exactly what happened," I told him.

The shock of my words silenced them all.

"Wait, you're getting around to it?" I blurted out as his words were starting to sink in.

I didn't think he believed in marriage and was trying to figure out how the hell I was supposed to explain that one to my parents. *Oh yeah, my very conservative, traditional father, by the way, I'm pregnant and living with him. But we're never actually going to get married, because of something you can't possibly understand, and I can't exactly tell you about anyway, that is far stronger and more important than marriage.* That would go over splendidly.

His hand went to his pocket almost subconsciously.

My eyes widened.

"You have it on you right now?" I asked in shock.

"Well, ask her then. What are you waiting for, son?"

James turned to face me as I tried not to freak out, and then he smirked. That smile made me relax.

"With all due respect sir, you gave me your blessing once before and I hope to hell you will again, but I'm going to reserve asking her for when the time is right and not under pressure to do so. But make no doubt, I do plan on marrying your daughter. I've loved her since the moment I first met her. We may not have handled everything well when we were young, but this time will be different. It has to be, because there is nothing I won't do for my family."

He was talking to my dad, but he was looking at me as he spoke.

I smiled and nodded, then let him kiss me right in front of the two of them.

Mom started dabbing at her eyes and fussing over the pizza. Dad was suddenly quiet as he watched us.

"Well, come on, let's eat. I assume you're staying for dinner, James?"

"Yes ma'am."

"Should have ordered a second pizza then. I remember how this boy eats," Dad teased, and I realized that everything was going to be okay.

James
Chapter 23

I still felt bad for leaving Katherine to deal with her parents alone, but at least I'd gotten there in time to turn things around. I hated that a call had to take priority over my mate's needs, but sometimes that was just par for the job. Knowing that didn't make me feel like less of an ass when she opened that door and I saw how upset she had been.

By the end of the night her parents were actually excited about the baby, though, and happy to see me back in her life. I hadn't really known what to expect from their reaction, but it cracked me up to know they'd remained Team James all along.

Moving us into Pack territory, at least for the time being, really was helping. Though I wasn't ready to admit that to Thomas.

I'd even gotten to spend the entire next day escorting Katherine around Collier as she followed up on those child well-check calls. Knowing everything she knew now; she had a better understanding of the cases she was tasked to work on, and I was happy to see there was no trouble brewing for her.

I enjoyed getting to spend another workday with her.

And today we'd both taken the afternoon off for a very important doctor appointment. I had never been to a human doctor before and aside from what I'd seen on television, I had no idea what to expect.

"Would you relax. It can't be that different from you going to see Doc."

"I don't just go see him, Katherine. We don't really get sick," I whispered. "There's no annual checkup or anything. I only go if there's an injury that needs tending to."

"Really?" she asked looking surprised. "You never get sick?" I shook my head.

It was almost as if I could read her mind as fears started to creep in. She leaned over to whisper in my ear.

"Is this okay? Will she somehow know, you know?"

"It's fine. Even if she were to run a genetic test, it would be really hard for her to tell anything at this stage. It's just a thriving little baby in there. I promise."

"Not a pup?" she whispered back, causing me to laugh.

"Katherine Carter, you can come back now."

I got up to go with her, but the lady stopped me.

"We'll just be a few minutes getting her settled in and then you can come back when we're done."

I assumed this was normal, but Katherine stopped.

"No. I want him there for all of this."

"Are you sure?" she asked.

"I'm positive."

The nurse pursed her lips but nodded. Without another word we were led back to a small room. I hated feeling confined like that. Ironic for a guy who had locked himself in a jail cell for two weeks.

"Just strip out of your clothes and put this robe on, open side to the front."

"Got it."

She shot me a look before leaving us alone in the room.

"That woman really doesn't like me for some reason."

Katherine just shrugged.

"She goes to church with my parents. I'm sure we'll be the talk of the year after this."

"Could have just used Doc."

"You are not getting out of this. Human doctors. Human hospital for this birth."

I looked at her like she was crazy.

"You're not even going to consider a homebirth?"

"Not likely."

"Do I get a say in this?"

"Also, not likely."

I groaned, but then she distracted me by taking off her clothes. I grew inappropriately hard seeing her naked body.

"Focus, James."

"Oh, I am," I assured her.

"Really? Here?"

"Is there a lock on the door?"

She smacked me with her shirt, but I grabbed it and pulled her onto my lap.

"You're going to get us in trouble."

I reached inside her opened robe and rolled her nipple between my fingers making her moan as I kissed her.

A knock on the door made her jump right out of my arms and wrap the robe tightly around her.

Fortunately, it wasn't the evil nurse this time, but the doctor whose smile was much more pleasant. There was even a twinkle in her eye that told me she knew exactly what I'd been up to.

"Hi, Katherine. I'm Dr. Webb. Are you ready to get started?"

"As ready as I'll ever be. This is James, the, uh, father."

"Well, let's go ahead and have you pee in this cup real fast and see what we're dealing with here."

They both left, but Katherine returned a few minutes later.

"Does she really think you would be here if you weren't pregnant?" I asked.

She rolled her eyes.

"It's standard procedure. When I come in for my annual checkup, I still have to pee in the damn cup to confirm I'm not pregnant, even if I tell them I haven't been sexually active at all."

"Annoying."

"It's fine. Just sit there and behave."

The doctor returned and I did as I was told. It wasn't easy though as she practically felt up my mate, first checking her breasts and then propping her legs up to check other things.

"Eyes up here," Katherine said. "It's awkward enough without you snarling."

"I'm not snarling."

"Yes, you are. You should see the look on you face."

"And done," Dr. Webb announced.

"That's it?" I asked.

She didn't reply right away as she checked something in the computer system and then turned back to smile.

"Not quite yet. By our calculations you should be about eight or nine weeks pregnant. Would you like to see your baby today?"

"Really?" Katherine asked.

I just nodded solemnly as she pulled out some sort of machine and started hooking it to a monitor.

"Just in case we have the dates off a little, we're going to do a quick internal sonogram, okay?"

"What does that mean?" I asked.

"It means you just need to sit back, hold her hand, and watch this screen right here. Otherwise, try to ignore me."

When I glanced over and saw the wand thing and suddenly realized what an internal sonogram meant, I found I was quite uncomfortable with the situation.

Katherine's hand ran through my hair to grab my attention. She was nervous but looked happy.

I ignored the doctor from there on and just focused on my mate.

Within minutes there was a swooshing sound filling the air and a weird little blob showing on the screen.

"Do you hear that? That's the sound of your baby's heartbeat."

Tears ran down Katherine's cheeks as I was overwhelmed by emotions myself.

"Our baby?" I asked reverently.

I kissed her hand and then her stomach as I stared at the screen in awe.

This was really happening.

"You're going to be a mom," I said, making her cry harder.

"You're going to be a dad," she reminded me.

I stood up and kissed her, tasting the salty tears on her lips. I didn't even care that the doctor was there and watching us.

She finished the exam and pointed out a few little things about our kid, like the arm and leg buds of the little alien looking tadpole blob. It was such a surreal experience.

When she was done, she cleaned off the equipment and then stood, smiling at us.

"Wow," I said, still just in awe of my mate and the tiny miracle we created together.

"Congratulations. I'm really happy for the both of you and look forward to seeing you again in about a month. You can go ahead and get dressed, then take this paperwork to the front and they'll get you checked out and give you a small gift to commemorate this moment."

"Thank you," I told her, rising to shake her hand before she left.

"Do either of you have any questions for me?"

Katherine just laid there staring up at the ceiling with a look of wonder on her face.

"Yeah, so sex is still okay for now, right? I'm not going to hurt the baby or anything?"

My mate's cheeks turned a dark red, but the doctor just smiled.

"I assure you, sex is perfectly fine and healthy at this stage. Barring no complications, it's fine at any stage."

"Thank God," I muttered as Katherine shot me a look, letting me know I should shut up now.

"Anything else?" Dr. Webb asked.

"Not right now. I'll be sure to keep a running list for our next appointment."

She chuckled. "You do that. I'm happy to answer them all."

"Thanks, Dr. Webb," Katherine said.

This time she left the room, leaving me alone with my mate. "Are you okay?"

"It's just real," she whispered. "This is really happening."

"Hell yes it is," I said, unable to stop grinning.

The robe she was wearing fluttered open when she turned slightly to look at me. I couldn't stop myself from reaching out to touch her.

She groaned. "I swear you have a one-track mind."

"It's just a good thing she was a female doctor. If that had been a male, I wouldn't have handled things as well. I already have a strong desire to mark you right here and now."

She groaned and shook her head but sat up and pushed my hand away. Changing back into her own clothes quickly, she grabbed the papers in one hand and my hand in the other and dragged me from the room.

We checked out quickly, taking the congratulations bag and the envelope with our baby's first pictures in it. With the next appointment scheduled, we were out of there and off to celebrate in our own way.

I raced home and then carefully helped her out of the car. I hadn't been kidding when I told her that if it had been a male, I wouldn't have handled things quite so well. Hell, I wasn't exactly handling it well seeing that woman's hands on my mate.

When she wasn't moving fast enough, I picked her up and threw her over my shoulder as I ran for the house.

"James! You barbarian, put me down," she screamed.

I didn't listen until we reached the bedroom, and I tossed her down on the bed. Immediately, I began removing her clothes as she laughed at me.

"Are you okay?"

"I will be."

"Can I expect this from every doctor appointment we have?"

"Probably. I'm not about to apologize for this," I warned her.

I couldn't get out of my clothes and inside my mate fast enough.

She gasped when I skipped over all foreplay and got right down to business as I pushed deep inside her.

Fully sheathed within her I stilled and let the calm of being connected to her in this way wash over me.

"Better?" she asked in a husky voice as she stared up at me.

"So much better," I confessed as I leaned down to kiss her.

I was perfectly happy to just be there with her, in her, but before long she wiggled beneath me and started to move.

"Tell me what you want," I told her.

"Is that a loaded question?" she asked with a scoff.

"No, I'm serious. Tell me what makes you feel good."

"You know what makes me feel good, James. You always know exactly how to please me."

Pride welled up within me.

"So do it!" she finally demanded.

"Yes, ma'am."

I grinned, knowing just what she needed, so I gave it to her in a fast and uninhibited roll in the sheets until we were both fully satiated.

Later, as we laid there in each other's arms, she sighed.

"Will this ever get old? Will I ever stop wanting you so much?"

"God, I hope not."

She laughed and smacked my chest.

"I'm being serious. Is this just the bond that makes me want you so badly all the time?"

"It's not just that," I insisted.

"But how can you know that for sure?"

I didn't like the direction these questions were heading. Was she second guessing things between us?

"I'm just trying to understand it all, James," she said, as if she could read my mind.

"I just know," I told her simply. "I don't know how to explain it. Yes, the bond can magnify my feelings, but they're still my feelings."

She nodded as she considered that.

"You haven't been spending as much time in your fur lately. Should you be shifting more? I don't want you to think you can't just because I can't."

"I'm fine," I assured her.

For now I was, at least. But she was right. I was used to spending far more time in my fur than most any other shifter I knew. That was largely because of her and having to sleep in my wolf form every night if I wanted to be close to her, and I desperately needed to be close to her.

I didn't have to do that anymore, but she was right. I couldn't just cut off my wolf cold turkey like that. No good would come from it.

"I'll see if the guys want to go for a run later," I finally told her.

She seemed surprisingly pleased by that.

"But now that I'm feeling a little calmer, what was in that bag they gave you at the appointment."

"I don't know," she admitted as she got up and walked out of the room to go and retrieve it.

I got up and followed her, loving how she hadn't felt the need to cover herself.

When we had been together before, she had been far more self-conscious, always covering herself, especially outside of the bedroom. She kept a damn robe hanging on the door. I had grown to hate that thing, preferring to see her like this.

She had needed more space and private time too. I tried to give her that some, but she really didn't seem to crave it the way I thought she had before.

She was a strong, confident woman now and damn if that wasn't an even bigger turn on. I was growing hard again just watching her walk across the room to sit next to me on the couch.

She carefully pulled out everything. There were a bunch of coupons, fliers, and pamphlets for things like Lamaze classes and a breakdown of common questions and answers. There was a copy of 'What to Expect When You're Expecting', and a picture frame that said 'Baby's First Picture'.

I picked up the envelope and opened it to find a stack of pictures from the ultrasound. There was one that clearly showed our little alien blob the best. I grinned as I took it and put it in the frame and then walked over to set it on the fireplace mantel right next to a picture of me and Katherine that seriously needed updating.

She got up and walked over to look at it.

"When did you put this picture out?" she asked about the one of the two of us.

"I never took it down," I confessed. "Look around, I never wanted to erase you. They just need some updating."

I pulled out my phone and snapped a picture of her.

She shrieked.

"James, I'm naked."

"My favorite."

"That is not getting printed and hung up anywhere. Are we clear?"

I frowned. "Fine. It's just for me then. Come here,"

I grabbed her around the waist and switched my phone to selfie mode as I took a picture of the two of us with our baby's picture in the background. I pointed to it with a grin, making sure to only get our faces in the photo and snapped the picture.

"Let me see."

I showed it to her.

"Send that one to me."

I did as she asked, happy that she wanted it too. Then I sent it over to our Six Pack thread to text the guys.

ME: It's official. I'm going to be a dad!

Within minutes responses started rolling in.

EMMETT: Congrats man. Unfortunately, she looks a lot like you with that weird-shaped head.

WYATT: That's not her head. That's a foot.

AUSTIN: You're both idiots. That's her butt, right?

THOMAS: Wait, how do you know it's a girl already?

AUSTIN: Jealous since Lily always makes you wait for the actual birth?

THOMAS: I'm serious. You can find that out already?

CLAY: No, you can't. And I think it's going to be a boy.

ME: No way. It's a girl.

CLAY: You don't know shit.

WYATT: If Thomas is any indication, all the Six Pack is destined for girls.

EMMETT: I think it would be cool to have a Six Pack little legacy league.

I chuckled.

"What?" Katherine asked.

"The guys think we're having a girl, but Clay's hoping for a boy."

"You think we're having a girl," she reminded me.

I shrugged. "Just a hunch."

She scowled and shook her head. "I think it's going to be a boy. Clay's right."

As she said it, she reached down and held her stomach. My mouth went dry. She was carrying my baby. The reality of that once again struck me like lightning.

Katherine
Chapter 24

James and I had fallen into a comfortable routine and, when I didn't let myself really think about things, everything was great. But when I was left alone and everything that had happened started to sink in, I struggled with so many questions left unanswered.

Morning sickness had set in, becoming a normal part of my everyday routine. I was tired of feeling like crap all the time. I was also sick of being weepy and emotional. Everyone told me it was normal pregnancy hormones, but it felt like hormones on steroids to me. There was no way this was normal. No one would ever have more than one child if this was normal.

My parents wanted to visit us, but we were still living at James's house. Was it safe for them to even come here? I didn't know, so I just put them off.

I wasn't scared of the wolves, but should I be? Everyone seemed so nice, and I was making friends like I'd never had before, but there was always this part of my brain reminding me that I didn't fit in here.

Tonight, James was on call and staying at the station late. That left me to my own demise with everything crashing in on me.

I grabbed my phone and called Lily.

"Hey, girl. What's up?"

"Are you busy tonight?"

"Katherine, what's wrong?"

"Nothing. I just don't want to be alone."

"Well, I just put the girls down and Thomas is still at the Alpha House working late. Why don't you come on over here?"

"Is that okay?"

"Of course it's okay. Have you been here before?"

"No."

"Okay, texting you the address now. See you in a few. Oh, and don't knock. Just let yourself in."

"Thanks. I'm on my way."

Within minutes I was sitting outside Lily's house second guessing my decision to call her in the first place. This was stupid. What could she even do or say to help me through all of this?

When she knocked on my window, I jumped and may have screamed a little.

"Are you coming inside or just sitting out here all alone?"

Embarrassed, I got out and followed her into the house.

"Take a seat and spill it."

"What?"

"Whatever you're thinking. Whatever's bothering you. Lay it on me."

"When I stop and think about things, it freaks me out."

"You mean us, the wolves?"

"All of it. You guys said James would be quick to claim me. I still don't fully understand what that means, but it hasn't happened."

Lily just listened until I stopped talking. I told her everything, all my fears, all my questions, all of it. I didn't hold anything back.

When I was done, she just hugged me.

"I can't even imagine how hard all of this is for you. And I understand all your questions. Some of these things you really just need to talk to James about."

"He gets, well, worried, and I don't want to send him into a rage again or anything. Those freak me out."

"Yeah, I get that. But I told you, if you just go to him, no matter how hard that seems, just touch him and he'll calm down, I promise."

"I know. It's crazy, but it works."

"What's really bothering you?"

"He hasn't even tried to claim me. We haven't even talked about it. Why hasn't he done that if it's so important for a shifter?"

"I don't know. Maybe he's worried that you won't be able to seal the bond."

"But I don't even know what that means. Will you explain it to me? How do I seal the bond?"

She laughed. "Well, it requires a blood exchange."

"Excuse me."

She pulled her shirt to the side and showed me her neck where a bite mark looked almost like a tattoo on her skin.

"Thomas bit you?"

"Yes. I know it sounds gross, but it's not. It's like the most orgasmic feeling you will ever experience."

I ran my tongue over my teeth, wondering just how hard I'd have to bite him to cause a mark like that.

"When did he do that to you?"

"Years ago. It's a permanent mark, Katherine. When you seal your bond, you'll carry James's mark."

I furrowed my brow as I tried to imagine it.

"Okay. I can bite him. No big deal, right?"

"It's a very big deal. Our wolf canines are called forward and used to pierce the skin."

"But I don't have wolf canines."

"Which is why I said James might be worried about trying. If he bites you and you can't bite him back it would cause an unrequited bond."

"And that's not good, I take it."

"No, it's not."

I sighed. "I don't know how to fix this."

"It's sort of new territory for everyone. But James is optimistic that you wouldn't be his true mate if it wasn't possible to completely seal your bond."

"He said that?"

She nodded.

"Maybe I just need to take the lead then and let him know that it's okay. I can do that."

She gave me a comical look.

"What? I can do that."

"I love you, Katherine, but this is a two-party thing. Go home and talk to James about it."

"He's on call. And when I'm left alone my mind sort of turns against me and makes me want to run away from all of this."

"Maybe that's why he hasn't tried to seal your bond. Did you think about that? If he senses your hesitation, he's not going to push you. He's just not that kind of man."

"I know. Okay. Good. This is good. Thanks, Lily. I think I've got it from here."

"You do?"

"Yeah. I need to get home and prepare."

"Oh boy. Um, are you sure you're good?"

"I'm great." I got up and hugged her. "I'll talk to you later. You're a really great friend. Thank you."

As I was leaving with a new mission in mind, Thomas walked in.

"Katherine. Is everything okay?"

"Never better. You have the best mate in the world."

"I do. Thanks."

"Goodnight."

I went back to my car and drove home. James was there pacing across the living room.

"Are you okay? Where were you?"

"I'm fine. I was just over at Lily's talking to her."

I went to him and placed my hands on his chest.

"Are you okay?" I asked him.

He gave me a quick kiss.

"I am now."

"Long day?"

"Yeah. Not a bad one, just a long one."

I started taking off his clothes as we talked. He stopped and raised an eyebrow at me.

"What are you doing?"

"Just helping you get more comfortable."

When I had him naked, I took my clothes off too.

I was nervous but determined.

Unable to keep my eyes off of his neck, I wrapped my arms around him and pressed myself to him, and then I bit him.

James jumped back making me squeal.

"Ow. What are you doing?"

"I'm trying to seal our bond, damn it."

I growled in frustration and then the tears started to flow as reality set in around me.

"Oh God, I can't do it. I'm only human."

I ran down the hall, into our bedroom, and then locked myself in the bathroom. I sat down on the floor and cried.

James knocked lightly.

"Katherine, are you okay?"

"I'm fine," I lied. "I'm just going to take a bath."

Just so I wasn't completely lying, I started a hot bath and sunk down into the steamy water.

I was never going to be able to seal myself to him. This wasn't going to work. What was I even doing here trying to live amongst wolves as if I belonged here. I didn't feel like I belonged anywhere. The ache that thought caused in my chest was undeniable.

Overwhelmed with emotions and stupid hormones, I cried until I was completely exhausted and then I started to snooze.

When I awoke, I was in bed wrapped up in James's arms. I had no idea how I'd gotten here, but knowing he had obviously cared for me in my sleep made me love him even more.

I was so torn. I knew I wanted to be with him. There was no doubt in my mind that I loved him and he loved me, but we were from two different worlds, and I felt torn between them.

Closing my eyes and just relaxing in the peace and comfort only he could provide, I drifted back off to sleep.

Awaking for a second time, I found myself alone in the dark just before sunrise.

"James?" I asked, but when I rolled over, I saw a note on his pillow.

Work called. Had to go in. Can we talk tonight?

I sighed. I knew he was worrying about me. Hell, I was worrying about me. My life felt like a complete mess, and I didn't know how to fix it.

I was told that when we sealed our bond things would settle, but I didn't know how to do that. I'd tried and it didn't work.

Pulling myself together, I got dressed for the day and left the house. It was still early so I called Mom to see if she wanted to have breakfast. Of course she was already up. She got up with my dad every day to see him off to work.

"I'm just finishing up breakfast now. Why don't you come here? There's plenty."

"I'll see you in a few minutes."

Dad was on his way out when I arrived.

He gave me a quick kiss on my cheek as we passed.

"Both my best girls this morning. It's going to be a great day," he told me.

I couldn't help but smile.

Inside I found Mom sitting at the kitchen table scrolling through her phone. She smiled when she saw me and then frowned.

"Katherine, you look terrible."

I sighed. "Rough night."

"Is the morning sickness still getting to you?"

"Yeah," I said, even though that was so far down the list of what was bothering me it wasn't even funny.

"You should call your doctor and have her prescribe something."

"I see her again next week. I'll ask then."

"How are things with James?" she asked.

"Good." It wasn't a lie. Everything was great with James and I, minus that part where I couldn't complete the bond with him and all. I couldn't exactly explain that to my very human mother though.

"Are you settling in okay over in Collier?" she asked.

"Yeah. Everyone's been surprisingly great and welcoming. I've even made some great friends there."

"That's fantastic dear. They can be a closed off bunch, but I'm sure they have their reasons for it. They are certainly a tight knit group, but I know a few of them to be wonderful people."

"You know people from Collier County?" I asked, careful not to slip up and say Collier Pack.

"I do. I have a sweet friend there, Cora Collier. Have you met her? We've been friends for ages and still have lunch a few times a year, usually around the holidays."

"I don't think I've met her."

Mom laughed, "Well I doubt she'd be running in your circle, but you might know her children. Let's see, there's a bunch of them. Lizzy is the oldest, then Ruby, no, I think Clara, Peyton, Shelby, Maddie, and then little Thomas."

My jaw dropped and I started to laugh. "Little Thomas? I don't think he's all that little anymore."

"So you do know him?"

"Yes, he's good friends with James and I've become close with his, um, wife, Lily."

I was going to have to watch myself when talking outside of the Pack. It would be so easy to slip up and say mate instead. I suspected that things like that were why they kept to themselves so tightly, well that and the obvious part about not wanting their secret to get out.

Finding out a pack of people that could shift into wolves and other animals was the kind of thing nightmares were made of. I tried not to let myself think about that or irrational fears would creep in again.

Before my mind started to wander off in that direction, I smiled at Mom and helped myself to a piece of toast.

"I just can't believe my baby is having a baby."

"Are you happy to be a grandmother?"

"Thrilled."

She got up and left the room and then returned with a shopping bag. Inside was a bunch of small infant toys and two gender neutral sleepers.

"Mom!"

"Well, I don't know if it's a girl or a boy yet, but I just couldn't resist. I tried to stay away from clothes, but these were too cute to pass over."

I pulled out each item with a smile.

"This is great. Thank you."

"I know your dad gave you both some grief about not at least getting engaged, but that is not our grandbaby's fault. And sometimes, things happen. You and James, that's your business. I can't guarantee I can keep him out of it, but I'll try. But a baby, that's a precious gift from God under any circumstance, and we are going to love him or her with all our hearts."

I cried as I hugged her.

"Thanks, Mom. I really needed to hear that."

"Is everything really okay with you and James? I'll admit, I was surprised to see the two of you back together."

"If I hadn't been so stubborn, it would have happened a lot sooner. I know I told you guys that he broke up with me, but I was the one that pushed him away. I was just scared by the intensity of my feelings for him and a lot of that is being dredged up again thanks to these stupid pregnancy hormones."

Mom smiled knowingly. "I like to think that there's one perfect someone out there somewhere for each of us, and James seems to be that person for you. If only you could see how you light up in that boy's presence."

"I do?"

"You really do. He brings an inner strength and certainty to your life that I haven't seen in a long time. Oh, your father's probably right and I just read too many romance books. I can't help it. I'm just an old romantic at heart and couldn't be happier to see the two of you back together again and starting a family of your own."

Her words stayed with me as I went about my day. She had no way of knowing about true mates, yet that desire to find the one person in this world who completes you isn't just a shifter thing. We all search for that missing piece of our hearts.

Maybe it's because books and movies capitalize on it, or maybe there's something valid and true about it. Just maybe, humans and shifters aren't so different after all.

I was still puzzling over it hours later when Allen popped into my office.

"Hey, I was wondering if you wanted to grab drinks after work tonight."

"Why? What's up? Is the Bradley case giving you some grief?"

He gave me a funny look. "Do I need a work reason to want to have drinks with you now?"

"Oh. Oh! Shit. Um, there's probably something you should know."

"What's that?"

"I'm seeing someone."

"Is it serious?"

"You could certainly say that. We're having a baby."

I knew that he struggled with boundaries and wouldn't stop pressing me for yet another disastrous date if he'd set his mind to it again. So I'd just blurted out the first thing that popped into my head.

It certainly wasn't how I had planned to announce it, but once it was out there, I couldn't rein it back in.

"You're pregnant?" he yelled, causing the entire office to stop what they were doing and get up to come and hear this for themselves.

I rubbed my temples, not wanting to deal with this right now.

"Yes, I am pregnant. Did you all hear that okay?" I laughed. "This is not how I planned to tell everyone, but there you go. I'm pregnant."

There was something powerful in those words. They made me feel strong and proud. I was unmarried, unmated, and pregnant. No matter what happened in my personal life it would always be me and this baby against the world, and I was ready to own up to that.

Much to my surprise, most of my colleagues were thrilled to hear it. Everyone came by to congratulate me while Allen went back to work to lick his wounds. Poor guy. If Mom was right, there was someone, somewhere out there just for him too, but it most definitely was not me.

It was time I started blending my two worlds in a way I could. So I pulled out my phone and sent the picture of me and James with him pointing to the sonogram picture of our baby to my printer, and then I pulled out an old frame tucked in the back of a desk drawer and proudly put it up on my desk.

I had enough secrets in my life, these two shouldn't have to be one of them. No one had to know what James was to know he was mine.

James

Chapter 25

My on-call shift couldn't end fast enough. Katherine was overly emotional, and I was worried about her. Last night she'd fallen asleep in the tub, and I'd had to let myself in and then carry her to bed. She looked exhausted and I knew she'd been crying.

We needed to talk. She had tried to bite me. I knew Lily must have tried to explain things to her. It had caught me off guard and I hadn't reacted well to it.

In hindsight it was kind of funny.

Still, it made old fears resurface that just maybe she couldn't seal our bond. I pushed those thoughts aside. There had to be a way. There had to. She was my true mate. I was certain of it.

I put in a call to Peyton for a special dinner order that I picked up on my way home. Steak, fettucine alfredo, and asparagus. There was fresh bread, too, plus raspberry chocolate cheesecake for dessert. All things Katherine loved.

The table was set, candles lit, everything looked perfect and romantic. I was even wearing dress pants and a button-down shirt, though I did forego a tie.

Waiting for her to come home was the hard part, but much to my surprise, she arrived earlier than I expected, and I realized I was nervous. I was ready to lay everything on the line, but I feared she would turn and run. Was I crazy for wanting to drag her into my world, one she didn't fully understand? Probably.

I needed her to know this was going to have to be her decision and hers alone. I'd even gotten the memory serum from Emmett. How the hell he'd gotten his hands on it was beyond me, but I wanted Katherine to understand she did have options.

Her earlier arrival was probably a good thing. I hadn't quite worked myself up to pacing just yet.

"What's all of this?" she asked.

"I thought a nice dinner in would do us both some good. Plus, we need to talk."

"About last night?"

I nodded. "About a lot of things."

She sighed. "Okay. Everything smells wonderful."

"Then, let's eat. I don't know about you, but I'm starved."

I helped her to her seat and then brought over the plates I had already prepped and left warming in the oven.

"Careful, the plate's a little hot."

"Wow. This is amazing James. I could get used to this."

My heart lurched in optimism feeling like we were at least off to a good start.

Katherine had been a little hot and cold lately. Her uncertainty was evident. I just didn't know what exactly she was uncertain about. She had tried to seal our bond in her own way, so that was promising. Still, I was a nervous mess going into this dinner.

"How was your day?" I asked.

"Good. I had breakfast with Mom. She's already started shopping for the baby."

I groaned. "Already?"

"Yes. It was really cute. Just some toys and a couple of sleepers that would work for a boy or a girl. She was asking if we were going to find out the gender before birth, and I wasn't sure how to answer that. Do you want to know?"

I shrugged. "I'm fine either way. Do you want to know?"

"I'm not sure. Waiting just might drive me crazy, but the surprise would be fun too."

"I guess it's something we should think about then. It's still too soon to find out anyway, right?"

"Yeah, it is, but the weeks seem to be flying by and a part of me just wants to yell, 'Slow down!' But I know that's not going to happen. Oh, and my office all knows about you and the baby now. Allen sort of asked me out again and I had to put a stop to it, so it all just came out."

I was surprised to hear it, but happy.

"At least I don't have to rip his throat out."

It was meant to be a joke, but the look of horror on her face told me she didn't get it.

"Sorry. That sounded barbaric. I didn't mean it like that. It's sort of our way of saying kick his ass or something."

"Should I be worried about my safety around a pack of wolves? I mean I know you would never purposefully hurt me, but what about the others?"

I suspected questions like this would surface eventually. She'd seemed to be taking everything in stride. It was bound to happen at some point.

"One of our most sacred vows is to never harm a human in our fur. In general, we just avoid humans as much as possible. In this world that's not exactly an easy task. As you know, I'm still called into a human court from time to time. We still shop in the human stores. The world isn't as small as our territory lines, but we do tend to keep to ourselves a little more. We have major consequences for hurting a human. You're probably the safest person in all of Collier Pack."

"So everyone has full control of their wolves when shifted?"

I considered that a moment, not wanting to scare her with my answer.

"Everyone here is very much in control of their wolf. We do have the ability to relinquish control to our animals, to turn off a piece of our humanity, but even then, there would have to be something very wrong with the wolf for it to become a danger to humans."

She nodded like she understood.

"Have you ever turned off your humanity and given full control to your wolf?"

I froze, not expecting that question but knowing I needed to be a hundred percent honest with her.

"Yes, I have."

"Why? When?"

I sucked in a breath and forged on.

"When you broke up with me. I couldn't handle it and I took to my fur for a few weeks out on the range. I submitted completely to my wolf. Thomas found me and coaxed me back."

"Weeks? Did you kill anyone?"

"No, not a person. I did mutilate a couple cows in the process. I'm not proud of it, but it happened."

"Did you eat them?"

I nodded. "Cows, rabbits, deer, whatever I had to. I don't make a habit of hunting and eating raw, but I can't honestly say I've never done it."

She looked down at her rare steak on her plate and poked at it with her fork.

"Is it much different than a rare steak?" she surprised me by asking.

I laughed. "Honestly, I don't know. I try not to think about it, it just is what it is."

She nodded and then shrugged as she cut off another piece of steak and popped it into her mouth.

Smiling, I ate a little more too.

"This is really good," she complimented.

"For a minute there I wasn't sure you were going to be able to eat with the whole hunting talk."

Her nose wrinkled in a cute way.

"My dad's a hunter. I don't get squeamish about stuff like that."

"Good to know. Do you have any other questions or concerns you want to talk about?"

She seemed to hesitate for a moment, and I didn't think she was going to speak up but then she did.

"Will our baby be safe here?"

"Yes. Absolutely. The Pack protects our own and this child is pack. Even if you decided you don't want to be with me and would rather raise her in the human world, the Pack would always be watching after her from afar."

She considered that.

"I have a choice to raise her in the human world? How would that even work at this point?"

I gulped hard.

"You always have a choice, Katherine. If this is all too much for you and you want out, I can give that to you."

It broke my heart to say those words, but she had to know that this was her decision, her choice.

Her brow furrowed as she watched me.

"But you said your wolf would always pine for me."

"That's true."

"And the girls told me what that could do to you, to your wolf."

I hadn't considered that.

"I'm sure that's true too. I could never do that to you. Besides, I know now, that's not something I could ever just forget."

"Actually, you can. There's a serum that was created by a human faction who protects my kind. We call it a memory serum. In cases of emergency where we've been accidentally exposed to humans, it can be used to erase those memories. You'd still know we were together. I'd still be the father of this child. But you wouldn't remember anything about the Pack or about shifters. You'd go to living your life in the dark."

"Why are you telling me this?"

"Because I've seen how you've been struggling lately. I know this can't be easy for you, and I only ever want whatever is best for you. So you need to know that you do have options."

"Would it take away our bond?"

"I think for you, it might."

"But not for you?"

"There's nothing that can stop it for me. It's said that the mating call is a choice and there is a way to sever even a true mate bond, but it's been researched for many, *many* years and no one can say exactly how to do that. You don't need to worry about me though, babe. We're talking about what's best for you and our baby."

Her mouth dropped open and then closed as anger crossed her face.

"What about you?"

"I don't matter here. I'm a survivor and I'll be fine, always watching from a distance, back to your guard dog if need be. The point is, you do have a choice in this."

"And you think this is the answer? I should just take this memory serum and erase you? Erase us?"

"God no! That's not what I'm saying at all."

"Then what *are* you saying?"

"I'm saying that this has to be your decision and yours alone because for me, you aren't just my true mate, my fated mate, my destined mate, or whatever you want to call it. Left up to me, I will choose you every second of every day for the *rest* of our lives. I choose you. I choose us. You are my chosen mate, Katherine."

Tears welled up in her eyes.

"What's it going to be? All in or all out from here on?"

I held my breath as I waited for her response holding up the small vile that I knew had the power to destroy me.

"That's it? The memory serum stuff?"

I nodded. "This is it. It's yours if you want it. Your choice, Katherine."

"Then get that shit out of my house. I don't ever want to speak of it again. I love you, James. I may get scared or freak out from time to time, and I'm definitely going to be overly emotional with all these baby hormones thrown in, but I'm yours. I choose you. That's never going to change."

"Thank God."

I set the serum down and was across the table pulling her from her seat within seconds. My lips crashed down on hers, reassuring myself she was real. She was here. She was mine.

Things heated between us quickly as her hands fumbled for the buttons on my dress shirt. At the last second, I stopped and blew out the candles on the table before lifting her in my arms and started to carry her back to the bedroom.

"Shit. Wait. Stop."

She growled in protest, making me smile.

"There's more?"

I gave her a quick kiss and dropped down to one knee as I fumbled for my pocket to retrieve the small jewelry box I'd been carrying around with me for just the right moment. Maybe there wasn't exactly the perfect time, but after all that was said, I desperately needed to hear her say yes.

She gasped.

"James Blakely, is that the two-carat princess cut diamond ring I turned down the last time you asked me to marry you and have regretted every day since?"

"Um, yes? Is that bad? Should I have bought a new one?"

"No! That's my ring! Now ask me again already."

I chuckled. "I'm getting there."

She gave me an impatient look as she held out her hand.

I slipped the ring onto her finger and then kissed her hand.

"Katherine Carter, will you make me the happiest man alive and be my wife?"

"Technically yes, but more importantly, I'm your mate."

"God, I love you."

I stood up and pulled her back into my arms to kiss her once more.

This time I swooped her up into a cradle and carried her to bed as she continued to admire the ring on her finger. My ring. It wasn't the same as leaving my mark on her, but it was a start.

"I don't want to wait to get married. I want to do it right away. I know it's not the same, but it is the human way of claiming you as my man for all the world to see."

"Whatever you want. I'll even wear a tux if that's what makes you happy."

She shrugged. "Or you could just wear your uniform."

I laughed. "My uniform?"

"What? You're super sexy in uniform. Don't even pretend like you don't know it."

I shrugged. "Whatever you want."

"What I want is you. Always and forever."

I took my time, carefully undressing her, and then laid naked beside her.

"I've always been yours and I always will be," I assured her.

I kissed her lips then across her cheek stopping to nibble on her earlobe before trailing more kisses down the column of her neck.

Her hands gently caressed my back as she cocked her head to one side fully exposing her neck to me.

I gulped hard, feeling my canines suddenly descend. This was it, the moment I'd equally been waiting for and dreading. I didn't know if she could reciprocate and seal our bond, but I couldn't wait a second longer to mark her as mine.

I kissed the spot I'd already chosen and then let my canines pierce her skin, claiming her as mine forever.

She gasped and then she moaned.

A sharp prick pierced through my skin followed by a slight sting of salty tears.

She did it! I didn't even know how it was possible, but she did it.

Keeping this sacred connection, I wrapped her legs around me and slid inside. For one perfect moment we were fully joined as one. Nothing could ever separate us again.

She moaned and sucked on my neck as she started to move.

A sort of frenzy took over and I couldn't possibly be deep enough in her. I wasn't even sure what was coming over me, but I had to have her. I needed to thoroughly make her mine.

I pulled out and then thrust back inside her.

Her nails scraped down my back.

Everything felt like more. My need was stronger than ever. My desire for her was almost uncontrollable. I felt high on the taste of her blood in my mouth as I branded my soul to hers and claimed her body as mine forever.

Her teeth disappeared as she pulled back and cried out my name.

"James! Oh God, don't stop. I need you so badly."

I let my own teeth withdraw as I sucked on the spot that now marked her as mine.

I wanted to howl out in victory. We'd done it. We'd sealed our bond despite all obstacles.

"Katherine," I moaned, finding her lips again as I continued to pound in and out of her.

Her legs wrapped around my waist. She was so impossibly tight around me. I'd never felt anything so perfect.

She was close, so close. I could feel it. With each thrust she squeezed me tighter, dragging me with her towards her climax.

"James," she panted. "James."

"Eyes open, babe. I want to watch you come."

Her eyes widened in surprise as she shattered apart in my arms, pulling me right along with her. The way the light danced across her eyes in a dozen different shades was mesmerizing.

"Did you feel it?" she asked as she tried to catch her breath. "It was like a miracle."

I smiled and nodded, holding her tight.

"I did it. I really did it," she said proudly. "I don't even know how it happened, but you bit me and it just seemed like something otherworldly overcame me and I did it."

There were tears in her eyes as I started to kiss her cheeks.

"I didn't know how it would work, but I never doubted us for a second."

She hugged me tight.

"That was amazing."

"You're amazing."

"I'm yours now."

"Always and forever."

Katherine

Epilogue

Five weeks later.

"Do you take this woman to be your lawfully wedded wife?"
James looked deeply into my eyes and grinned. "I do."
"And do you, Katherine, take…"
"Yes. I do. I really, really do."
Those in attendance chuckled.

If it had been left up to me, we would have just gone to the courthouse the day after he'd proposed and we had sealed our bond. This all seemed ridiculous to me now. We were bonded and nothing was more important than that.

But James had insisted on a real wedding, saying something about how it was his chance to publicly claim me for all the humans.

Whatever. My mate definitely had a bit of hopeless romantic in him.

I'd finally met his parents in the process. They were nice and welcoming, though still not entirely comfortable with me being a human and all. Still, they agreed to come to the wedding, as did his sisters and their families. The Six Pack and the entire Collier County Sheriff's office were there, along with my family, a few of their friends, and my staff at work.

Mom wasn't exactly pleased with the rushed wedding plans, but I'd at least agreed to an actual wedding. She'd worked day and night for the last few weeks to transition their backyard into a magical wedding venue.

Everything was beautiful, but all I saw was my handsome mate standing before me. He beamed back at me as we exchanged rings.

"You may kiss your bride," the Reverend told him as cheers went up all around us.

James's lips on mine felt like home.

"Mine," I whispered.

He hugged me tightly.

"Mine," he echoed.

"May I present Mr. and Mrs. James Blakely."

Our friends and family clapped. Mom dabbed at her eyes, and I think Dad may have too, though he'd never admit it.

James walked me proudly down the small aisle and we were assaulted with hugs when we reached the end.

"Okay, we have to hurry," he whispered.

"Go," Mom said with a scowl.

James took my hand and we ran off to our awaiting car. I was still in my bridal gown and he in his uniform.

Mom wasn't exactly thrilled by our plans to cram everything into one day, but it was all working out just fine. They were busy transitioning the yard from a wedding chapel to the reception. Food and drinks would be plentiful, and we'd be back to join the party just as soon as we got through our big appointment.

I checked in at the front desk when we arrived, getting a few weird looks shot my way. I didn't care. This was my day.

"Any changes to make since your last appointment?" the receptionist asked.

"No," I said.

"Yes," James corrected.

I rolled my eyes and grinned.

"He's right. It's no longer Katherine Carter. It's Katherine Blakely now."

"Much better," James praised, wrapping his arms around my waist as his hands splayed out across my already growing belly.

"Congratulations," she said with a grin. "You can head back now. Room three."

"Thank you."

Dr. Webb already knew our plans and that we were in a hurry. The gown was laid out, but as I stripped out of my wedding dress, it was hard to ignore the hungry look in my husband's eyes.

"We don't have time," I warned him.

"We'll make time," he said, moving to lock the door.

"James!"

"Katherine," he growled.

Before our standoff ended, there was a knock on the door that made us both jump. He growled in frustration.

"Later," I promised with a wink.

"Okay, kids. I take it everything went well today?"

"It's done," I assured her with a grin. "He made me an honest woman."

James snorted.

"Let's get through this quickly so you can get back to your reception." She laughed and shook her head.

It was insane, but exactly what I wanted. James and I had decided that it was important to both of us to include our child in today's festivities, so our wedding reception was doubling as a baby shower.

Neither of us really loved being thrown in the spotlight so might as well kill two birds with one stone.

Dr. Webb did a quick basic check and then readied the ultrasound machine.

"Just so we're clear, you do not want to know the sex of your baby now, right? We're still going with the plan of a gender reveal,

"Yes," we both said.

She grinned. "I love this. Wish I could take the afternoon off and join you."

"You know you're welcome if you can make it," James assured her.

"Unfortunately, I have two women in labor today and have to make my rounds after this. But I want to hear all about it at your next appointment."

We both agreed as she applied the gel to my stomach and pressed the magic ultrasound wand to it so we could see our baby.

"Wow, she's gotten big in there," James said in wonder.

"She?" Dr. Webb asked with a smile. "Are you sure about that?"

He shrugged. "Just a hunch."

"How about you?" she asked me.

"I say it's a boy, but he's been so insistent it's a girl that I almost believe him."

"Well, my lips are sealed."

She took some measurements and snapped a few pictures. The sound of this kid's heartbeat filling the silence of the room was the greatest noise I'd ever heard.

"Okay, I'm done. I can't wait to hear all about this. Good luck."

"Thanks."

When she left, James pulled out a duffle bag and handed me the outfit I'd chosen for the reception slash baby shower.

He also started to strip out of his uniform for something more comfortable.

I caught him eyeballing the door.

"We're on a time crunch here. And I am not going back there smelling like sex."

"You're already knocked up. It wouldn't be that much of a shocker."

I playfully smacked him. "James!"

"What? I'm just saying."

"Save it for the honeymoon."

He grinned from ear to ear.

We were flying out for Hawaii in roughly twenty-four hours. He'd truly gone all out for such a last-minute wedding. One week all alone with my man. I wasn't even certain we'd see the beach, but I didn't care. All I needed was him.

"Come on, slow poke," he teased.

I finished dressing; he packed up our things; and we left, but not before stopping by the nurse's station where she gave us two confetti cannons and an envelope with pictures from the ultrasound.

"Thanks," we said.

"Congratulations," she yelled to our retreating backs.

In no time at all, we were back at the house I'd grown up in where everyone important to us was patiently waiting.

The DJ stopped and made an announcement when he saw us.

"Let's welcome back Mr. and Mrs. Blakely."

I took James's arm as he led me to the front of the room and accepted the mic the DJ held out for him.

"Katherine and I just want to say thank you for showing up and supporting us today. It's been a bit of a whirlwind kind of day, but lately that seems to be our life."

I chuckled, knowing just how true that was.

"As you all know, we have a lot to celebrate today. Today we joined together in this thing called life and vowed to face whatever comes, together. Well, there's a new addition coming fast."

I beamed proudly, but the others laughed knowingly.

"Today we'd like you all to join us for a gender reveal as we're about to know if there's a little girl or a little boy on the way."

"It's a girl," Austin yelled out.

"I mean, that's what I think," he confessed.

I shook my head.

"Team Pink," Thomas chimed in.

"Stop egging him on. It could be a boy," I insisted, making them all laugh again.

"Okay, well, no need to argue it any longer. If you all will help us count down from ten, we'll find out together."

"Ten... nine... eight... seven... six... five... four... three... two... one..."

I held my breath and twisted the cannon just as James did on his.

Blue confetti flew through the air.

"I told you!" I squealed.

James shrugged and grabbed me around the waist as he swung me through the air and kissed me a dozen times for all to see.

"Thomas, you better watch those daughters of yours because we have a little Six Pack legacy in the making now," Emmett yelled out.

Mom and Dad walked over and hugged us. James's parents did too.

"Do you have a name picked out already?" his father asked.

"We do," James said handing me the mic as everyone settled down to hear.

"Carter Thomas Blakely," I said proudly.

My dad beamed proudly.

"Carter is a good strong name."

"One we wanted to carry on into the next generation," I told him as I kissed his cheek.

Tears pricked my eyes as Thomas walked up and hugged James.

"I'm honored, truly."

Lily hugged me. "Congratulations."

Looking around at all the faces surrounding us, my heart swelled. Maybe life wouldn't be the easiest for a human living in a shifter world, but this was exactly where I belonged. Wedged between two worlds is where I found mine.

*****

Thank you for reading His Chosen Mate.

Ready for more? Check out Can't Be Love for Thomas and Lily's story.

Of if you're brand new to my PNR World, and can't wait for more, try starting at the book that began it all with Kyle & Kelsey in One True Mate.

And be sure to keep reading for a special announcement regarding His Fierce Mate, book 3 in the Six Pack Shifters series. (hint, it's Austin's story!)

Julie Trettel

Dear Reader,

Thanks for reading His True Mate. If you enjoyed Clay & Winnie's story, please consider dropping a review. https://mybook.to/SixPack2 It helps more than you know.

For further information on my books, events, and life in general, I can be found online here:

Website: www.julietrettel.com

www.facebook.com/authorjulietrettel

www.instragram.com/julie.trettel

https://www.bookbub.com/authors/julie-trettel

http://www.goodreads.com/author/show/14703924.Julie_Trettel

http://www.amazon.com/Julie_Trettel/e/B018HS9GXS

Sign up for my Newsletter with a free Westin Pack Short Story!
https://dl.bookfunnel.com/add9nm91rs

Love my books?
Join my Reader Group, Julie Trettel's Book Lover's on Facebook!
https://www.facebook.com/groups/compounderspod7

With love and thanks,
Julie Trettel

Sneak Peek
His Fierce Mate

I don't exactly have "a job" around Collier Pack. I tend to have my hands in a lot of things. Human doctors would most definitely diagnose me as ADHD. I get bored and tend to find trouble if I stay put in one place too long. Fortunately, I'm tight with the Alpha. He's one of us, the Six Pack. He understands this about me. I'm never not working and don't slack on my responsibilities; it just varies day-to-day what I'm doing. I like variety.

I like variety in my women too. As I watch my friends all falling to their true mates, I have to wonder if that'll ever be me. As nice as it sounds that there is one person out there fated to be with me forever, someone that completes me, I have to wonder, is that really for me?

I couldn't even fathom settling down like that, waking up to the same woman every day. Heck, I like my space and my freedom and rarely have sleepovers to wake up next to anyone. I am a perpetual flirt and that just isn't going change. The more I think about it, the more I'm not sure this true mate stuff is for me.

That is until one fateful night out on the range when an angel appears.

I'm not being dramatic here. That's her name, Angel, my true mate, the one who is about to destroy everything I thought I knew about myself.

Austin & Angel coming July 14, 2023 in His Fierce Mate

*****

Pre-order your copy today! https://mybook.to/SixPack3

More books by Julie Trettel!

Westin Pack
One True Mate
Fighting Destiny
Forever Mine
Confusing Hearts
Can't Be Love
Under a Harvest Moon

Collier Pack
Breathe Again
Run Free
In Plain Sight
Broken Chains
Coming Home
Holiday Surprise

ARC Shifters
Pack's Promise
Winter's Promise
Midnight Promise
iPromise
New Promise
Don't Promise
Forgotten Promise
Hidden Promise
All-Star Promise

Westin Force
Fierce Impact
Rising Storm
Collision Course
Technical Threat
Final Extraction
Waging War

Six Pack Shifters
His Destined Mate
His True Mate
His Chosen Mate

Westin Force Delta
High Risk
Nothing to Chance

Bonus Westin World Books
Ravenden
A Collier First Christmas
Shifter Marked and Claimed
Panther's Pride: The Shifter Trials
Christmas at Kaitlyn's Place

More books by: Jules Trettel!

Armstrong Academy
Louis and the Secrets of the Ring
Octavia and the Tiny Tornadoes
William and the Look Alike
Hannah and the Sea of Tears
Eamon and the Mysteries of Magic
May and the Strawberry Scented Catastrophe
Gil and the Hidden Tunnels
Elaina and the History of Helios
Alaric and the Shaky Start
Mack and the Disappearing Act
Halloween and the Secret's Blown
Ivan and the Masked Crusader
Dani and the Frozen Mishaps

Stones of Amaria
Legends of Sorcery
Ruins of Magic
Keeper of Light
Fall of Darkness

The Compounders Series
The Compounders: Book1
Dissension
Discontent
Sedition

Julie Trettel

About the Author

Julie Trettel is a USA Today Bestselling Author of Paranormal Romance. She comes from a long line of story tellers. Writing has always been a stress reliever and escape for her to manage the crazy demands of juggling time and schedules between work and an active family of six. In her "free time," she enjoys traveling, reading, outdoor activities, and spending time with family and friends.

Visit

www.JulieTrettel.com